Amy Cross is the author of more than 250 horror,
paranormal, fantasy and thriller novels.

OTHER TITLES
BY AMY CROSS INCLUDE

THE HAUNTING OF LOTHAM LODGE

THE GHOSTS OF ROSE RADCLIFFE BOOK 3

AMY CROSS

CONTENTS

THE HAUNTING OF LOTHAM LODGE

CHAPTER ONE

MORNING LIGHT SHONE THROUGH the stained glass window set into a large white door. The pattern on the window showed a rose in varying shades of red and green, while two smaller panels showed a rich red salmon and an orangey-red squirrel.

A moment later two shadows fell across the window from outside. A key slid into the lock and jiggled around for a moment, before slowly the handle turned to reveal first Rebecca Pearson and then a young girl – no more than nine or ten years old – holding a small backpack in her hands.

"Welcome to our home, Rose," Rebecca said with a hint of nervousness in her voice. She waited for a moment before gesturing into the hallway. "It's okay. You can go inside. It's your home too now."

Clearly filled with fear, Rose slowly stepped forward into the house. Looking around, she saw various paintings on the walls and a large mirror hanging over a small table. A set of carpeted stairs led up to the top floor, but for a moment all Rose could do was slowly turn to look at the various doors leading off into other parts of the house. More than anything, she was struck by the smell of polish – and perhaps of various other cleaning products too – and by the fact that the Pearsons' house seemed so very neat and tidy.

Behind her the door bumped shut, and Rose immediately flinched and turned to look back.

"We're home!" Rebecca called out with a smile as she slipped out of her coat and hung it on the rack. "Rose, do you want to take your coat off?"

Not really knowing what else to say, Rose set her backpack down and then slowly removed her coat. A moment later Rebecca took the coat from her hands and the young girl, still feeling extremely confused, simply picked up her backpack again. Everything about this new house felt completely strange and unfamiliar, and she couldn't help but feel as if she absolutely didn't belong in any possible way. Already she was fighting the urge to turn around and run away, although she had no idea where she was supposed to run *to*.

"Is that Rose?" another voice said, and a moment later Jonathan Pearson made his way through from the kitchen, still wiping his hands on a tea towel. "Hello there, Rose. It's good to see you again."

He held a hand out.

Rose inspected the hand for a moment before slowly giving it a shake, but she was still looking past her hosts and watching the various open doors. Her eyes were filled with a sense of suspicion and she seemed almost to be holding her breath, only taking gulps of air when they were strictly needed.

"I've got everything ready for a nice lunch," Jonathan said, stepping back and heading to the end of a nearby corridor. "Why don't you two come through and join us?"

Us?

As soon as she heard that word, Rose felt another flicker of fear.

"It's okay," Rebecca whispered, placing a hand on the girl's shoulder and giving it a gentle squeeze. "She doesn't bite."

Rose looked up at her.

"You two are going to get along like a house

on fire," Rebecca continued, offering the most comforting smile she could possibly dredge up from the depths of her soul. "I promise."

***

"So what do you prefer?" Jonathan asked a few minutes later, setting several cartons on the round table in the corner of the kitchen. "We have orange juice, blood orange juice, grapefruit juice, tropical fruit juice, cranberry juice and..."

He had to turn the last carton around to check.

"Vitamin boost juice," he muttered, furrowing his brow. "I'm not sure what that one's all about."

Staring at the cartons, Rose had no idea which of them she should pick.

"Oh, and let's not forget the apple juice," Jonathan added, setting a seventh carton down. "Nothing beats good old fashioned apple juice, not in my experience. Now just pour yourself something while I sort out the scrambled eggs."

Still bemused, Rose thought back to the small glass of strange yellow liquid she'd always been offered back at the center. Breakfast there had been in a communal room where she'd shared tables with the various other girls waiting to be re-homed, while breakfast back at Marlstone Hall with her mother had been a quiet and very formal affair. Here at the Pearsons' home, however, breakfast seemed much fuller and happier, with a whirl of activity as both Rebecca and Jonathan took various plates and items of cutlery from cupboards and drawers. Meanwhile brightly-colored paper napkins had already been folded and left on the plates.

And then...

And then there was Alicia.

Having barely dared to look her in the eye so far, Rose finally turned and saw that Alicia had already fixed her with a determined stare. Having already heard a huge amount about Alicia from Rebecca and Jonathan, Rose knew that the girl was about two years her senior and was very much accustomed to having her parents all to herself. Blonde-haired and with a somewhat unwelcoming look in her eyes, Alicia had so far said all of about five words – and those had only escaped her lips because she'd been forced by her parents to speak.

Rose had spent enough time at the re-homing center to know when she'd made a bad first impression.

"Are you girls okay over there?" Jonathan called over to them. "Alicia, why don't you help

Rose pick some juice?"

"Don't you know what kind of juice you like?" Alicia asked, still staring at Rose.

"I..."

Hesitating for a moment, Rose felt as if anything she said was going to be wrong. At the same time, she knew that indifference wasn't an option and that she *had* to pick one of the cartons. She'd never realized that such a simple choice could have such huge ramifications.

"Just pick one," Alicia added. "It's not that hard."

Turning to look at the cartons, Rose was unable to shake the sense that she was walking straight into a trap. The cartons all looked cheerful enough, and in truth she really didn't mind which of them she ended up drinking from. She just wanted to avoid causing any trouble, and more than anything else she was desperate to find the one carton that would make Alicia like her more. She wasn't sure exactly what she'd done to upset the other girl, but she could only assume that it was here mere presence that was causing the problem.

"You and Alicia are going to get along so well," Rebecca had told her so many times. "I think it'll be good for her to have someone else her own age in the house. She's grown up all by herself and I really want her to make some new friends."

Now, after swallowing hard, Rose decided to try smiling. She managed just about, but as the seconds ticked past she realized that Alicia was offering nothing in return.

"Did you figure it out?" Jonathan asked.

"Let them be," Rebecca whispered, trying to keep her voice down. "You don't have to fuss all the time."

"Just pick one," Alicia said again, somehow managing to sound even more bored and unimpressed than before. "It doesn't even matter."

Realizing that she simply had to get on with the task at hand, Rose reached out for the carton of orange juice. At the last second, however, she spotted the faintest hint of an increased scowl in Alicia's eyes and she immediately understood that she was about to make the wrong choice. Somehow in her mind she'd already convinced herself that this was some hugely important test, that her entire future in the Pearson household was going to be determined by her very first choice of fruit juice. One of the cartons was clearly correct while the rest would mark her out forever as some kind of idiot.

She felt as if she'd been thrust into some kind of game, perhaps a little like chess – except the pieces were all fruit juice cartons, the board was the breakfast table and the rules hadn't been explained.

"Whatever," Alicia said suddenly, grabbing the carton of tropical fruit juice and pouring herself some, before putting the carton back in place.

Immediately taking the carton for herself, Rose poured some into her own glass. She had no idea whether she'd made the right decision, but she knew it was too late to turn back now so she finished pouring the glass and then she set the carton back in the row with the others. Glancing at Alicia, she waited for some kind of signal that she'd made the right choice, and then she picked the glass up and took a sip.

The taste, she realized, wasn't bad at all, but more than anything she was relieved that she'd finally made her move. She downed the rest of the glass before setting it down onto the table, and then she waited in hope that she might finally have made some kind of breakthrough.

"Great," Alicia muttered under her breath as a steaming bowl of scrambled eggs was placed down between them. "Such a little copycat."

CHAPTER TWO

"I THINK THEY'RE GETTING on okay," Rebecca said several hours later, standing at the sink and looking out at the garden. "I mean... it's not bad for the first day, at least."

Over by the steps, Alicia was poking at some dirt while Rose was sitting nearby and simply staring down at her own hands. Having been told to go outside for a little while, the two girls showed absolutely no sign that they wanted to play together, and if anything they seemed to be trying to pretend that they were alone.

"It'll get better," Rebecca added, although there was a strong hint of doubt in her voice. "It *has* to get better. It'd be crazy to expect them to become best friends on the first day."

She hesitated for a moment longer, before turning to see that Jonathan was sorting through his briefcase on the kitchen table.

"Have we made a terrible mistake?" she asked finally. "Jonathan, I know you had your reservations when I said I wanted us to foster Rose, and I know I insisted it'd all be okay and that she'd fit perfectly into our family but..."

Her voice trailed off for a moment as she thought of all the things that might go wrong.

"What if this is the worst possible choice?" she continued. "Alicia's always been quite... solitary, and I really thought that having another girl roughly her own age living here would help. Instead she almost seems to be going deeper into herself."

"It'll be fine," Jonathan replied, clearly preoccupied by the task of reorganizing various papers in the briefcase.

"What if they take her away from us?" Rebecca asked. "This is only a temporary arrangement so far and they warned us that she might only be with us for a few months. Jonathan, what if she ends up getting move again? What if by trying to help her, we're only making things even worse? At least at the home she had some kind of stability after she left Marlstone Hall. I don't want her to be bouncing from one place to the next."

"She's not a puppy."

"You know what I mean."

"It'll be fine."

"But what if it isn't?" she asked, struggling to stay calm now. "I'm starting to think that I should have listened to you a little more. You warned me that I was maybe being unrealistic but I kept insisting that we could make it work. I could tell that the case manager wasn't convinced either, but I suppose they're so desperate to get as many kids re-homed as possible that they decided to take a chance. But what if we're making Rose's life so much harder? It's not like her first meeting with us was exactly relaxing, either. What if living with us only serves as a daily reminder of all the awful things that happened at Marlstone Hall?"

"It'll be fine."

"What if she misses her aunt too much? At least she knows now that Ida *is* only her aunt. That has to have screwed her up massively, and we're not the best people to help her navigate that problem. Jonathan, what if we've rushed in to try to help her but instead we're only going to ruin her entire life?"

"Rebecca," he replied, making his way over and kissing her on the cheek, "it'll be fine."

"But -"

"I'm just sorry that I have to go to this

conference," he continued. "It's such lousy timing, but when they asked us to take Rose a week early, there was nothing I could do."

"I know," she murmured.

"Are you sure your mother can't make it?" he asked.

"She won't be back from holiday until next week," Rebecca reminded him, before pausing again. "I can look after them for a few days. That's not a problem. I just wish I could find a way to make them get along better." Glancing out the window, she saw that Alicia and Rose were now sitting even further apart on the steps. "They could be such good friends," she added, close to tears now. "If only they'd give each other a chance."

"Do you know what you need to do?" Jonathan replied. "You need to stop worrying and overthinking it all so much."

***

"It's going to be a disaster," Rebecca said, flat on her back in the dark bedroom and staring up at the ceiling. "I can feel it in my bones. Raising Alicia has been hard enough, why did I ever think that I could cope with fostering?"

"Hmm?" Jonathan said, rolling over to look

at her, having *almost* managed to fall asleep.

"Fostering is so different to parenting your own child," she continued, clearly wide awake. "All the books I read made that point, but I naively assumed that I'd be able to handle it. Can you believe that? How could I possibly have had so much mis-placed confidence? Everyone tried to warn me but I just went storming ahead in the mistaken belief that pure good intentions would push me through."

"Rebecca -"

"And the worst part is that I might end up ruining two childhoods in the process," she added, as if she hadn't even heard his attempted interruption. "There's not just Rose to consider. What if Alicia starts thinking that I don't love her enough? What if she thinks that I'm trying to replace her? What if -"

Suddenly a hand settled softly against her mouth.

"You're a wonderful mother to Alicia," Jonathan said gently, "and you're already doing a great job with Rose. *We're* doing a great job. You're not in this alone, remember? The case manager warned us that the first few days might be extremely challenging, and so far it's going a lot better than I expected. Sure, Alicia finds it weird suddenly having a kind of little sister living here, but frankly I'd be more worried if she didn't. And Rose, as we both know all too well, has been through some very difficult things over the past year or so. The fact that she's settling in as well as she is means that we must be doing something right."

"But -"

"And the fact that you're stressing so much is completely normal too," he continued, with his hand still resting on her mouth. "We're both going to look back one day and laugh at this moment. Taking Rose on is an enormous responsibility and it's a good thing that we recognize that. Again, I think that all this fuss and self-doubt is just part of how the whole thing works. You just need to trust the process."

He paused for a moment.

"Listen, I've been thinking," he added, "I might call John Warden in the morning and tell him I can't make the conference after all. I can say I've got the flu or something."

She turned to him, and in the moonlight she saw something strangely comforting in his eyes. She desperately wanted to accept his offer, but at the same time she knew that he'd been planning for this particular conference for over a year. She'd sworn that taking Rose in wouldn't damage their professional lives, that was one of the big promises she'd made all through the application process, and she told herself that she had to hit the ground running.

"You're not canceling," she told him.

"If -"

"You're *not* canceling," she said again, much more firmly this time. Reaching up, she moved his hand away from her face. "I can handle the girls for the weekend," she continued. "Yes, it's faintly terrifying right now, but I can do it. And this conference is important for both of us, it's the first time you're going to present a paper where you even hint at the possibility of..."

Her voice faded away for a few seconds.

"You know what I mean," she added. "I read the pre-print, Jonathan. The part where you acknowledge the possibility of things we don't understand in the paranormal field is... it's going to ruffle a lot of feathers."

"Don't worry about that right now," he replied.

"I'm serious," she continued. "I know you ummed and ahhed about including that section. To be honest, for a while I thought you might leave it out entirely. When you told me you were going to include it, I was so relieved. I know you're still not completely convinced about what happened at Marlstone Hall, but I'm just glad that you agreed to include that section in our paper. I wish I could be there to present it with you."

"It's nothing," he told her, rolling onto his back again. "We should both get to sleep, though. I've got a long drive tomorrow and you... well, I can't even begin to imagine what your day's going to be like, but I'm fairly sure it's going to be hectic."

"I'm going to take the girls to the zoo," she replied. "I figured it'd be good to take them out and maybe help them bond a little. Plus it'll tire them out."

"Sounds like a wonderful plan," he murmured, already closing his eyes again. "Everything's going to be fine, Rebecca. Just you wait and see. From this point on, it's all... plain..."

Within seconds he was fast asleep again, snoring gently, while Rebecca remained wide awake and continued to stare at the ceiling. Already her mind was once again filling with all sorts of fears, and she still couldn't quite shake the fear that taking in Rose Radcliffe might have been a terrible mistake for everyone concerned.

CHAPTER THREE

"THAT WAS A FASCINATING paper," Humphrey Craven said a few days later, holding a glass of red wine as he stood in the hotel bar. "Jonathan, I've honestly never heard anything like it. What you and your wife experienced last year at Marlstone Hall... I mean, I read about it of course and I heard the rumors, but to hear it from your own mouth..."

"I just hope I did it justice," Jonathan murmured, checking his watch for the umpteenth time.

"Are you sure you won't have a glass?" Humphrey asked. "It's just cheap hotel plonk, of course, but it does the job."

"I have to hit the road soon," Jonathan replied. "Long drive. Next time, perhaps."

"You're not staying for the after party? You surprise me, Jonathan. You must know that the last nights of these conferences are always the most fun. Last year we had to fish poor Henry Chapman out of a pond." He paused for a moment. "You know, there was one thing that surprised me a little about your paper tonight. I heard a few whispers that you and your dear wife were going to make some rather startling suggestions."

"Never believe rumors," Jonathan said uneasily.

"I heard you were going to leave open the possibility of... peculiar goings-on."

"I'm really not sure what you mean."

"After old Delaney lost his mind and ended up dead," Humphrey continued, "some people whispered that you and Rebecca were tempted to believe that something supernatural might have happened at Marlstone Hall. You must have noticed that your presentation today drew a decent crowd. This might seem barmy, but some people thought you were actually going to propose further study of the ridiculous idea that ghosts might be real. In fact, at one point toward the end you seemed a little uncertain, almost as if you were considering the idea."

"I presented the paper I wanted to present,"

Jonathan explained, checking his watch yet again. "Listen, I'm going to have to hit the road. My wife and I have taken in a... boarder, and I really don't want to leave them alone for any longer than necessary. You won't think I'm rude if I bugger off, will you?"

"I'll think that you're missing out on some rather poor wine," Humphrey replied, holding his glass up. "It seems to develop a film if it's left undisturbed for any length of time. My doctor keeps telling me I should give it up, but I always tell him that a life lived without wine isn't a life worth living at all. That usually shuts him up. Of course, it helps that I know the old chap's a bit of an alcy himself. If you think *my* nose is a little burgundy in color, you should see that fellow's hooter! It looks like someone has glued a ruddy beetroot on the front of his face!"

"I'll be in touch," Jonathan replied, setting his glass of lemonade down and turning to leave the bar. "Good luck with the rest of the night."

"I meant what I said about your paper!" Humphrey called after him. "It was first class! I'm just glad you didn't embarrass yourself by waffling on about ghosts! Oh, and good luck at home with your new Border Collie! Such wonderful dogs!"

***

"And in other news," the voice on the radio continued as Jonathan steered his car around another bend in the dark road, "the funeral was held today for the American astronaut Neil Armstrong. Armstrong, who died last weekend at the age of eight-two. A pioneering figure in the -"

Hearing a buzzing sound, Jonathan looked down at the passenger seat and saw that his phone was ringing. As soon as he spotted his wife's name on the screen, he felt a flicker of fear. The voice on the radio was still speaking, talking about the death of Neil Armstrong, and for a few seconds Jonathan told himself that he could simply pretend that he hadn't heard the phone going at all.

Finally, however, he pulled off at the side of the road and turned the radio's volume down, and then he tapped to answer the call.

"Hey," he said, with a trace of concern in his voice, "I'm about halfway. I should be home a little after midnight."

"How did it go?" Rebecca asked on the other end of the line.

"Fine," he said cautiously, before hesitating. "Why? What did you hear?"

"Nothing," she continued airily.

He felt himself relaxing just a little.

"I've been run off my feet all day with the girls," she explained, "but I've just put them to bed. I let them stay up a little later than planned to watch a film together. They're not exactly best buddies yet, but at least they acknowledge each other. So how did the presentation of our paper go? How did people react to some of the stuff at the end about Marlstone Hall?"

"It went... well," Jonathan replied, choosing his words with care. "I think people were generally onboard with it all."

"That's a relief," she murmured. "Even the stuff about paranormal activity? I've been so worried about how everyone would respond to that part of the paper being revealed. Was there much backlash?"

"I wouldn't say that I picked up on any backlash," he told her, before pausing for a few seconds. "Actually, in the end I decided to -"

"That's a miracle, then," she said, interrupting him before he could confess that he'd cut out a large section at the end of the presentation. "I was braced for ridicule, but I guess it's a good sign if people took the whole thing seriously. Then again, we spent a lot of time trying to bolster the evidence for our claims, so maybe I shouldn't be quite so surprised. But there must have been *some* pushing back, right? There's no way a hall full of our peers just accepted our proposition about there being real ghosts at Marlstone Hall."

"It's... tricky to say," he admitted. "I had to shoot off pretty much straight after the panel. I didn't even have time to grab a lemonade in the bar."

"I'm so relieved that we've finally put this idea out there," she said with a sigh. "I know you weren't entirely convinced that it was the right time, Jonathan. I'm sorry if you feel like I pushed you to do it. To be honest, part of me even worried that you might back out at the last minute."

"What do you mean?" he asked tensely.

"Just that you might drop that part of the presentation," she continued. "Especially with me not being there. Thank you for keeping it all in, though. It means a lot to me that you were willing to take my ideas seriously and to support them even though I wasn't there in person."

"I should get going," he said awkwardly. "I'm parked by the side of the road in the middle of some forest, and to be honest I want to get to the next service station and see if there's any coffee on the go. Sometimes I feel like I spend half my life at service stations."

"I'll let you go," she told him, "but thank you again for presenting the paper the way you did. I have to admit, I'll be glad when you get home. It's been fun with the girls and they haven't been too bad, but I definitely think they'll react better when we're both around."

"See you soon," he replied, before cutting the call and setting the phone down.

For a moment he simply sat in silence. He knew he should have confessed the truth, that he should have admitted to his wife that at the last moment he'd cut out all the paranormal stuff from the presentation. Worried about being made to look like a fool, he'd stuck to the safer section about psychiatric issues and simple explanations. In truth, while he'd certainly been shocked by everything at Marlstone Hall a year earlier, over time he'd felt as if reason and logic had reasserted their hold on his mind, and he'd begun to ease back on any belief in the paranormal. Rebecca, meanwhile, remained convinced that there had been actual ghosts there. He just hadn't found a way yet to admit that he was going back to his original view.

Somewhere in the distance, a brief loud boom rang out.

Reminding himself that he had to tell Rebecca the truth about the paper before she found out from someone else, he reached out to start the engine. He could feel a sense of dread rising through his chest and he knew his wife would be disappointed – that she might even feel betrayed – but he told himself that he simply had to be honest with her and admit that he wasn't quite so sure about -

Suddenly he froze as he heard a woman's voice screaming somewhere nearby in the forest.

CHAPTER FOUR

STUMBLING AWAY FROM THE car, Jonathan finally reached the edge of the road and stopped for a moment to look out at the darkness of the forest.

He wasn't even sure exactly where the scream had come from, except that it had seemed very close. After just a few seconds, however, it had died out abruptly, and already he was starting to wonder whether he might have been mistaken all along. Was it not possible, he realized now, that the 'scream' had actually come from some wild roving animal and that in fact there was no cause for concern?

After all, he knew that foxes could make the most horrible sounds.

Then again, as he stood in the cold night air and waited for any further hint of a cry, he also realized that he was woefully ill-equipped to help if anyone *was* in trouble. As a chilly wind blew along the road and ruffled his tie, he felt a growing sense of relief as he heard nothing louder than the rustling of nearby trees. Finally, after perhaps a minute longer, he told himself that nothing was wrong and that he could simply get back into the car and drive away.

"Is... everything okay?" he called out cautiously, mainly to help himself feel that he was doing the right thing.

He waited, but nobody answered.

"Okay then," he murmured, turning and making his way back to the car.

As he climbed inside and started the engine again, he told himself that there was nothing else he could possibly do. He was certainly in no position to go stumbling around in the pitch-black forest, and anyway he couldn't even be sure which direction the supposed scream had come from. As for calling the police, he reasoned that he would simply be laughed at if he tried to drag some poor under-resourced copper out to stand in the middle of a remote road listening for weird sounds coming from the forest.

Easing the car back out onto the road, he set off again, and already he was returning his focus to the fact that he needed to tell Rebecca the truth. He knew he couldn't possibly have delivered the most ridiculous part of the presentation, the part that Rebecca herself had mostly written concerning genuine ghosts at Marlstone Hall; if she'd been at the conference with him, obviously he'd have let her read that part out, but he felt it was a little wrong to have expected him to propose *her* crazy idea.

Steering the car around another bend, he figured that -

Suddenly a figure stumbled out into the road, and Jonathan slammed his foot against the brake pedal with such force that the car barely came to a juddering halt in time.

Ahead of him, picked out by the car's headlights, stood an elderly woman wearing a dark green coat. She stared back at him with a shocked expression, before turning and looking back toward the forest.

Unbuckling his seat belt, Jonathan opened the door and climbed out.

"Are you okay?" he stammered. "I didn't hit you, did I?"

Seemingly not having heard him, the woman simply continued to stare at the forest.

"You just ran out," Jonathan continued. "I wasn't even going that fast. I certainly wasn't speeding. You know, you really ought to be more careful. You can't just stumble out into the middle of the road like that. I know there's probably not much traffic around this late at night, but still, you gave me a hell of a fright."

The woman checked her watch, glaring at it for a moment almost as if she was timing something.

"Did you scream just now?" Jonathan added. "I thought I heard... I mean, I might have been wrong, but I thought I heard someone crying out."

"Did you hear the gunshot?" she replied, turning to him.

"I'm sorry?"

"You must have done," she continued. "If you heard my scream, then surely you must have heard the gun going off. Please, tell me you heard it."

"Well, I -"

Thinking back for a moment, he realized that he *had* heard something a few seconds before the scream, even if – at the time – he hadn't quite realized that it had been a gunshot.

"Fine," she said with a heavy, labored sigh. "You don't exactly look like the attentive type. In fact, you've got the face of someone who misses quite a lot."

"I'm sorry?"

Checking her watch again, the woman turned and looked back into the forest. After a few seconds Jonathan realized that she was whispering to herself, and a couple of seconds after that he realized that she seemed to be counting. As much as he wanted to simply get back into his car and drive away, he couldn't help but worry whether this woman might have escaped from some kind of local psychiatric hospital.

"The lodge," she said finally.

"The what?"

"I need to get back to the lodge," she continued. "I'm so annoyed with myself for panicking like that, I should have held my resolve better. Now I'm behind schedule." She turned to him. "You're going to have to drive me."

"I'm sorry?"

"Drive," she said again, more firmly this time, before nodding toward his car. "I assume that vehicle belongs to you, doesn't it? I'm going to need you to drive me back to Lotham Lodge."

***

"It's just up here on the left," the woman – who still hadn't bothered to introduce herself – said as Jonathan continued to drive along the rough dirt road leading away through the forest. "You'll see it soon enough."

"Right," he replied, "and -"

"That's good," she continued, once again taking a look at her watch. "Okay, we're making up time now, I should actually be back a little ahead of schedule. It's my own fault for mucking about so badly after I heard the shot but, well, I suppose I shouldn't have assumed myself to be immune to such things. Even if I have to admit that I'm rather embarrassed."

"Right," Jonathan said again, just as he spotted the lights of a house up ahead. "If you don't mind, what -"

"Just pull up here," she added firmly. "Just to the right. There's a bloody big puddle in the middle of the driveway, it always collects when there's even a small amount of rain and then it takes forever to drain."

Still somewhat bemused by everything that was happening, Jonathan spotted the puddle glinting in a patch of moonlight. Taking care to drive around the offending patch of water, he swung the car round until he managed to pull up directly in front of the house, and then he cut the engine as he peered out at the building.

"You didn't have to come so close," the woman said impatiently, already unbuckling her seat belt. "You'll have a tough time getting out now. There's lots of mud over on the other side and if your wheels become stuck in it, you'll likely have a great deal of trouble getting out. I could call Wyn to come over with his tractor, but he wouldn't be able to make it until the morning at the earliest. You'd be well and truly stranded."

"Thank you for the warning," Jonathan said cautiously, still peering out at the house.

"You've been very helpful," the woman told him as she climbed out of the car. "You've saved me quite a bit of time. There's nothing else I require, however, so you can be on your way now. All that's left for me to do now is wait for the ghostly chap to show his face. Goodnight."

With that she swung the door shut and marched around the car, quickly heading up the steps and through the front door of the house.

"Did you say... ghostly or ghastly?" Jonathan called after her, but she'd already disappeared from sight.

Left sitting alone in the car, feeling utterly confused, Jonathan's first instinct was simply to start the engine again and set off. He certainly had no desire to linger outside some random house in the middle of the forest, yet at the same time he couldn't help but think back to some of the curious comments made by the woman. She hadn't bothered to actually explain what was going on; instead she'd simply barked a series of orders while making vague references to punctuality and – possibly, at the end – to a 'ghostly chap'.

As some lights were switched on inside the house, Jonathan again felt the urge to leave, yet he still couldn't quite bring himself to start the engine.

Finally he climbed out of the car and swung

the door shut, before walking up the steps and knocking. His mind was spinning and he wasn't quite sure what he expected to happen, but a few seconds later he heard footsteps and the door opened, revealing the same woman as before.

"Well?" she said, seemingly rather irritated by his interruption. "What are you doing still here? Why are you standing gormlessly on the step?" She waited for an answer. "What's wrong, has the cat got your tongue? I'm very busy so just get on with it. What do you want?"

CHAPTER FIVE

AS MOONLIGHT STREAMED THROUGH a window, the house stood in utter silence and darkness. Until, that is, one of the bedroom doors very slowly squeaked open and Rose leaned out to check that the coast was clear.

She waited, listening out for even the slightest hint that anyone else was up, and then she stepped out onto the landing with her backpack once again over her shoulder. Having waited and waited until a little after midnight, and having struggled to decide exactly what she was going to do, she'd finally come to a conclusion and had got dressed. Now she crept toward the top of the stairs again, and she felt more certain than ever that her best bet was simply to sneak out of the house and run away forever.

She had no idea where she was going to end up, but she supposed that she'd be able to think of something once she was on the road.

As she began to make her way down, she remembered a creaking loose board about halfway up the stairs. Expertly stepping over two of the boards, she managed to avoid making a sound as she tiptoed down to the hallway, and then she stopped again to make sure that everyone else was sound asleep.

Spotting her shoes near the door, she made her way over, but at the last second she heard her belly starting to rumble. In truth, since arriving at the Pearsons' house she'd eaten very little, mainly because of nerves but also because she was scared of seeming greedy.

She heard her stomach growling again, and then slowly she turned and looked toward the kitchen.

Although she desperately wanted to simply get going, she was feeling increasingly hungry and she remembered seeing an almost untouched chocolate gateau in the fridge. Telling herself that nobody would notice if she shaved off an extra slice, just to keep her going as she ran away, she began to creep on tiptoes across the hallway and over to the kitchen door. There she stopped again, still worried that at any moment she might be caught, and finally she made her way to the fridge and pulled it open.

Light immediately flooded out, filling her face. Seeing so much food inside, Rose was momentarily awed by the possibilities, but she quickly reminded herself that the gateau was by far her best bet. For one thing, a single slice had already been taken, so she reasoned that nobody would necessarily notice if she took some more. After all, she didn't want to be thought of as a thief. And for another thing, while there were plenty of healthier options, in that moment Rose *really* wanted a piece of chocolate cake.

Realizing that she needed a knife, she crept to the drawer and pulled one out. She hated sneaking about and she didn't want to upset Rebecca, but after just a few days she'd already come to the conclusion that she couldn't stay at the Pearsons' house. Heading back to the fridge, she reached inside and cut herself a small slice of cake, before quickly wolfing it down while still standing in front of the open door.

A few chocolate crumbs fell onto the floor.

Once she'd swallowed the last piece of cake, she looked longingly at the rest before telling herself that she couldn't possibly take more. Although she still felt hungry, she closed the door and turned to go back over to the sink so that she could wash the knife, but in that moment she was horrified to see a figure watching her from the doorway.

***

"I don't care if you tell her," Rose said a moment later, making her way to the hall and sitting at the bottom of the stairs so that she could put her shoes on. "Do what you want."

"But why are you running away?" Alicia asked, having followed her through. "Are you serious? Where are you even going to go?"

"I don't know."

"So what's your plan?"

"I don't know."

"But when you get out of the house," Alicia continued, "are you going to turn left or right? Are you going to go toward the center of town or to the edge? Are you -"

"I told you, I don't know!" Rose hissed, before looking up at the landing to make sure that Rebecca wasn't awake. "I'll think of something."

"You won't," Alicia replied. "There's nothing to think *of*. I could tell you were stupid, but I didn't think you were going to do something like this."

"I thought you'd be happy. I'm going to leave you all alone."

"Mummy won't be happy," Alicia told her. "Neither will Daddy. They were looking forward to you coming for weeks. You were all they could talk about."

"I'll go back to the home they got me from," Rose said cautiously. "At least there I wasn't bothering anyone."

"Who do you think you're bothering here?"

"You."

Alicia opened her mouth for a moment to reply, before holding back at the last second.

"You don't want me here," Rose continued. "It's okay. I know. You don't need to keep pretending."

"I didn't say that."

"I can still tell," Rose explained, before getting back to work putting her shoes on. Once she was done, she got to her feet with her backpack still over her shoulders. "I get it. You don't want to share anything so you want me to go away. If it was me, I'd probably be the same. I wouldn't want to share when I lived in such a nice house."

She turned and headed to the front door.

"You'll make them really sad," Alicia said suddenly.

Stopping, Rose turned to her again.

"You will," Alicia said with a shrug. "Especially Mummy. I think she always wanted me to have a brother or sister but..."

Her voice trailed off for a moment.

"I don't know. A puppy."

Rose furrowed her brow.

"What happened to you?" Alicia asked after a few more seconds. "Why did you have to find somewhere else to live? Mummy said that you don't have a family anymore."

"I had to go and live at a place while they looked for a new family for me."

"Why?"

"I couldn't stay at Marlstone Hall by myself."

"Is that where you lived before?"

Rose nodded.

"With your parents?"

Rose thought for a moment before slowly shaking her head.

"So where are they?" Alicia asked.

"I don't know," Rose muttered, clearly trying to avoid going into too much detail. "Do you really think Rebecca would be upset if I ran away? I thought... I thought maybe it'd make everyone happier."

"I think you should stay," Alicia said, even though she didn't sound hugely enthusiastic about that idea. "I think... I think it'd be too much fuss if you ran away, so it's better for everyone if you just try to like it here."

Rose opened her mouth to reply, but at the last second she heard a door opening upstairs. Before she had a chance to react, Alicia grabbed her arm and pulled her out of view, just as Rebecca emerged from one of the bedrooms and wandered tiredly into the bathroom. The two girls hid out of sight for a couple of minutes until Rebecca headed back through, and then they heard the bedroom door gently swinging shut.

Letting go of Rose's arm, Alicia crept over to the bottom of the staircase and looked up. She waited, worried that at any moment Rebecca might decide to go and check on the other rooms, but finally she allowed herself a sigh of relief.

"It's alright," she whispered finally, before turning to Rose. "I think -"

In that instant she froze, as she saw that Rose was standing completely rigid with her back against the wall, staring at her with wide-open eyes. Alicia's first instinct was that this was some attempt at a game, but after a couple of seconds she began to realize that something was wrong.

"Are you okay?" she stammered, stepping closer and grabbing her hand – only to immediately feel that Rose's skin was strangely hot and clammy. "Rose, what -"

"Tell him not to go in there!" Rose gasped as her body began to tremble heavily. "Tell him to stay out! He doesn't need to be there and he doesn't understand the danger! Tell him to stay out or -"

Suddenly she fell forward, slamming into Alicia before slithering down and landing hard on the floor. Rolling over, she started shaking violently as her eyes slid up to reveal only the whites. Saliva was frothing around her lips and although she seemed to be trying to say something, any words were catching in the back of her throat as she began to shake harder and harder. Now the back of her head was slamming repeatedly against the wooden floor, until Alicia rushed over and dropped down to her knees. Cradling Rose's head, she held her tight as she waited for the fit to end.

"Mummy!" she screamed. "Help! It's Rose! Something's wrong with her!"

CHAPTER SIX

"WELCOME TO LOTHAM LODGE," the woman said, stepping aside and watching as Jonathan stepped into the under-lit and distinctly gloomy entrance hallway. "Part of the Makepeace and Partington Estate."

Looking around, Jonathan saw dark wooden panels on all the walls and an array of rather dowdy still life paintings hanging between candle-holders. The place had a distinctly woody smell, too, and he couldn't shake the feeling that it hadn't been regularly used for a while.

"I'm sorry," he said after a moment, "what estate did you say again?"

"Makepeace and Partington," the woman explained again. "I know, it's a horrendous and very corporate name, but I'm afraid those are the times we're living in. This was the old hunting lodge. Back in the day, the great and the good would stay at the manor house for a weekend of hunting, shooting and fishing. It was the middle of those activities that required the use of the lodge. They used to overnight here when they were engaged in the hunting of deer and other animals far out in the forest. Why bother trudging back to the big house each night when they could just as easily camp out in the lodge?"

"It's quite fancy for a spare property," Jonathan pointed out.

"It's not really anything these days," she added with a wry smile. "The manor is used for weddings and corporate functions, but sadly the lodge has been left to gather dust."

Reaching out, she ran a fingertip along the top of a nearby shelf before holding up a gathering of dust.

"Quite literally, I'm afraid. Such is the fate of so many English country properties these days. It's hardly a novel tale. So much of our history is being left to quietly rot away."

"Are you the owner?" Jonathan asked.

"Me?" She stared at him incredulously for a moment, as if she was highly amused by that idea. "Heavens, no! I'm rather flattered that you could think such a thing, but I'm not a member of the landed gentry."

She hesitated, before stepping over to him and holding out a hand.

"Patricia Windermere," she added as they shook. "There was a time many decades ago when my family was something, but I'm afraid the fortune was frittered away by a combination of incompetents, gamblers and incompetent gamblers. Eventually my father was employed as a groundskeeper on this estate, but that was really just an honorary position. Everyone rather felt sorry for him, but when I came of age and he fell ill, I decided to make a go of it instead. I learned everything there was to learn – not from Papa, I hasten to add – and I rather fancy myself as a valued employee these days."

"And does your job require you to go sneaking around in the forest at night?"

Hesitating, she wandered over to the window and peered out at the moonlit driveway.

"It's midnight," he pointed out. "Slightly after. I can't imagine there's much hunting going on after dark."

"Not of the traditional variety, at least," she replied, staring out at the darkness for a moment longer before checking her watch as she turned to him. "These days my tasks are generally limited to arranging for various gardeners and technicians to attend the estate. The company that owns the property sees me as an amusing leftover from a more old-fashioned time, but – bless them, they keep me on and allow me to potter about. I generally pick my own projects but I shall be retiring later this year. And before I do so, I want to take one last shot at resolving the mystery of this lodge."

"Go on," he replied, having already accepted that he was going to be a little late home.

"Many years ago," she continued, "about a hundred years back, there was a gamekeeper here by the name of Maurice Wooden. Terrible name, I know. Anyway, it seems that one day he led a shooting party out to try to find some pheasants. Some members of the party were rather inexperienced, and a gun was unfortunately discharged directly into poor Maurice's face. They say there wasn't much left of him from the neck up, but it's rumored that he clung to life until the early hours of the following morning. Just a few minutes after 1am, to be precise."

"Unfortunate indeed," Jonathan mused.

"There were some rather unfortunate rumors that it was actually the master of the house who'd fired the fatal shot. Lord Makepeace was a fine marksman in his youth but he was prone to drinking too much. Apparently he mistakenly shot poor Maurice and then had his lawyers cover the whole thing up. Then, to add insult to injury, he behaved rather poorly toward Maurice's wife Anne. She worked as an artist at the estate at the time, during some restoration work. The whole thing would have been an utter scandal if the upper classes of the period hadn't been so terribly good at covering it all up."

"A somber story indeed," Jonathan admitted, "but I fail to understand what it has to do with anything that's happening tonight."

"This happens to be the anniversary of Maurice's death. The fourteenth of September. Well, he was shot on the thirteenth, but now we're past midnight so it's the fourteenth and that's the true anniversary. And ever since, there have been stories that on this one night each year, the poor chap's ghostly figure can be seen trudging back toward this very lodge."

"A ghost story," Jonathan said with a faint smile. "I had a feeling we were venturing into this kind of territory."

"You don't believe in such things?"

"I've had reason to ponder that very question a lot over the past year," he told her, "and... I might have begun to believe, but now logic is starting to take over again. I'm gradually returning to my previous position on the matter."

"Then why not test yourself fully?" she asked with a mischievous glint in her eyes. "It's less than an hour now. Why not stay with me until then and see whether poor Maurice makes another appearance?"

***

"You've probably gone to bed by now," Jonathan said as he stood in the lodge's old sitting room with his phone against one ear. "I just wanted to let you know that I'll be a few hours later than planned. Everything's okay, it's just that I've found myself in a somewhat improbable situation and..."

His voice trailed off as he wondered whether he could ever fully explain the strangeness of his encounter with the mysterious Patricia Windermere.

"I'll tell you all about it when I get back," he added finally. "I think you'll probably be rather enamored of the whole story once you hear the details. Just don't wait up, okay? I hope you and the girls have had a nice evening. I can't wait to join you and -"

Before he could finish, he heard a beep and he realized that his voicemail message was over. He briefly considered leaving another, only to tell himself that he should let Rebecca sleep instead. Slipping the phone away, he felt a shiver run through his body as he looked at the window, and he found himself wondering whether he might be making a terrible mistake.

"Did you get through?"

Turning, he saw Patricia standing in the doorway.

"I left a message," he explained.

"There's the old louche," she replied, stepping across the room and stopping to look up at a large painted portrait of a man with a dark mustache. "Lord Alfie Makepeace, late of this manor. The drunk who, if stories are to be believed, was responsible for Maurice's death. It certainly seems to be no coincidence that his family soon began to desert him."

"It's not a very flattering painting," Jonathan observed as he wandered over to join her.

"He was found dead in the kitchen," she told him.

He glanced at her.

"No, really," she continued, clearly able to tell that he didn't quite believe her. "Right under the stained glass portrait of himself, I believe. His former servant returned for his belongings and found him one morning. There were stories that he'd died of fright after witnessing Maurice's ghost returning one night, but of course one never truly knows what went on, does one? I checked it out, though, and the death certificate certainly makes fright sound like a possible cause."

"And has His Lordship's ghost ever shown up?"

"Not according to any of the stories I've

ever heard. But a gunshot is often said to ring out shortly before midnight each year, to signal the approach of Maurice's ghost, and I certainly heard something that sounded like a gunshot tonight. I must confess that in the darkness out there I momentarily lost my mind a little. Until my dying day, I shall be ashamed of that scream."

"You're lucky I showed up when I did."

"Oh, luck has nothing to do with it," she muttered, clearly irritated as she checked her watch. "Only half an hour now and then he should be here. I always promised myself that I'd come and see for myself and, well, this is likely my last chance. After all this time, I should like to know once and for all whether there's really a ghost here."

"I've got a feeling you're going to be disappointed," he told her.

"Perhaps, or perhaps not," she said darkly. "Either way, we shall find in half an hour from now."

CHAPTER SEVEN

A FOX CRIED OUT somewhere in the distance as Jonathan stood in the lodge's kitchen and stared up at the stained glass window. Someone long ago had seen fit to commission a rather large and complicated image of a man holding the carcass of a deer, although in the moonlight all the doubtlessly bright reds and oranges and yellows were rendered as darker tones.

What kind of man, Jonathan wondered, would want to be rendered forever in stained glass? He found himself imagining some inane, almost caricatured posh old English gentleman, high on a sense of self-importance. He knew the old Hartley quote about the past being a foreign country, and that sentiment had never seemed so truc as he tried to conjure up some sense of Lotham Lodge's former owners.

"That's him again," Patricia said as she stepped into the room.

"I assumed," Jonathan admitted. "He was certainly quite full of himself."

"Maurice's wife was the artist."

He half-turned to her as she made her way over to join him.

"Anne Wooden was one of the most renowned stained glass artists in the country," she explained. "She died a long time ago, of course, but her work can still be seen in some of the finest homes up and down the land. Of course, back then she was a woman in an industry dominated by men, but she seems to have never fought for fame or wealth or recognition. For her, the work itself was more than enough reward. It's said that even after her husband died, she stayed at the lodge to finish her creation. Some even claim..."

She hesitated, and when Jonathan turned to her he saw a hint of sadness in her eyes.

"Some even claim that her tears were mixed in with the pigments," she continued. "You see, Anne was a perfectionist who even insisted on creating her own colored glass right here on the site. She even had her own furnace installed here on the estate for the duration of the project. Since Lord Makepeace was desperate to show off, he would have footed the bill – I'm quite sure that it would have been mere pocket change for him. It's said that she experimented for more than two years, determined to find the exact colors that matched her vision. Have you ever dabbled with stained glass yourself, Mr. Pearson?"

"I can't say that I have," he admitted.

"It's a beautiful process," she told him with a slightly wistful tone in her voice. "I've never blown glass from scratch myself, of course, but I went to a two-day stained glass course once and found the whole thing fascinating. Cutting the glass was rather difficult, but assembling it and then completing all the finishing touches... I certainly enjoyed myself. I made a neat little image of a shining sun. Nothing too ambitious but it pleased me immensely. In fact, it's still at home today."

She paused again, before stepping forward and reaching up to touch the huge window, running her fingers across the lead strips.

"I can't imagine the satisfaction of doing the entire thing from scratch oneself," she said softly. "I'm no artist, Mr. Pearson, but I admire those who are. If I'm honest, I envy them a great deal."

"It sounds like you missed your calling," he replied, before glancing at his watch. "What time exactly do you think this ghost is due?"

"One minute past three," she said, glancing at him with a smile. "That's about twenty minutes from now. You're not getting nervous, are you?"

"What are all those hooks for?" he asked, trying to change the subject as he looked at some of the two dozen or so large metal hooks running along the far wall.

Something about the hooks sent a shiver through his bones; their sharpened tips hinted at a use that perhaps extended beyond the simple hanging of coats or bags.

"What do you *think* they were for?" she replied, clearly amused by his naivety. "This was a working kitchen on a country estate, in a hunting lodge no less. The carcasses of deer and other kills were hung in here ready to be butchered. Tell me, you're not one of those dreadful vegetarian types are you?"

"No, but sometimes I wonder about the meat industry."

"There's nothing so satisfying," she continued, walking over to some of the hooks and gazing up at them with a wistful stare, "as hoisting a warm deer carcass up onto one of these things." She looked down at the gutter that ran along the length of the room. "It was all done in here, you know. The chef would cut the animal open. Nothing – and I mean nothing – would be wasted. Of course, those days are long gone now. The estate's little more than an amusement park for people who want to experience ye olde England for a few days at a time."

She ran a fingertip against one of the hooks with obvious fondness, taking particular care to touch the slightly rusting tip.

"We won't get those days back again," she mused softly. "Not in my lifetime. More's the pity."

"So do you really believe that Maurice Wooden is going to show up tonight?" he asked. "With... what, with his head all blasted apart?"

"There are different versions of the story," she said, turning to him. "No two are the same, as you might expect. People are terrible witnesses, even to things that happen right in front of them. But that's the gist of it, yes. It's said that poor Maurice was such a devoted worker that he still comes back to the lodge to serve his master. Have you ever heard of anything more loyal and determined? And pathetic? The lowly servant must doff his cap to his master, even if death itself tries to get in the way."

"You don't approve?"

Pulling his phone out, Jonathan checked to see whether there was any reply from Rebecca, although he quickly told himself that it was a good thing if she'd simply retired for the night. Hopefully she and the children would simply sleep through the night, and in the morning he'd have an entertaining little story to tell them.

"I think I want to see for myself if it's all true," Patricia said firmly. "Anyway, it doesn't matter what either of us might think. In seventeen minutes, Maurice will either show up or he won't, and then we'll have our answer."

***

Reaching the top of the stairs, Jonathan looked both ways along the moonlit landing. He wasn't really sure what he was expecting to find, but he'd decided to fill some time by exploring the lodge and after a moment he wandered over to one of the nearby open doorways.

Looking through into the next room, he saw a double bed pressed against the wall and a large dresser over on the other side. He walked into the room and made his way to the window, and when he looked outside he saw nothing but the forest that spread out for miles and miles away from Lotham Lodge. For the first time he was struck by the utter isolation of the place, and by the realization that the lodge was truly marooned out in the middle of nowhere. Certainly there was no sign of any town or village, not as far as the eye could see.

Was the ghost of poor old Maurice Wooden out there now, already on his way? The idea seemed utterly ludicrous, yet Jonathan couldn't help but think back to everything that had happened one year earlier at Marlstone Hall.

"Did they find the other girl?" his wife had

asked once it was all over.

"Rebecca -"

"I know, I know," she'd continued, "you think that I was just stressed. And you might well be right, but I saw her so clearly. And she looked just like one of the evacuees in the photograph. Don't worry, I'm not saying that I saw a ghost, but I saw *something*. And then there's the fact that I somehow knew Rose was in that well. I can't explain it, but on some instinctual level... I just knew."

As much as he'd wanted to disagree with her, he'd slowly allowed himself to be talked around to her way of seeing things. After all, there had certainly been plenty of strange events at Marlstone Hall, and later Rebecca had even shown him a video that seemed to pick up an image of one of the ghosts. He'd spent the following year torn between belief and skepticism, although ultimately it had been the latter viewpoint that had won out, even if he hadn't yet admitted as much to his wife.

Fundamentally he was quite unable to believe in the unbelievable.

Rebecca, meanwhile, had begun to believe more and more in ghosts and spirits and all that sort of thing. Sometimes Jonathan admired her for opening her mind in a way that he found difficult, but there were moments when he worried that she was simply making herself look foolish. He'd nearly pulled out of their joint paper so many times, and in the end – with Rebecca suddenly unable to make the conference – he'd omitted the part that mattered the most to her. He felt bad, but at the same time... how could she possibly expect him to embarrass himself so publicly?

"Fifteen minutes, Mr. Pearson!" Patricia called up from the hallway, breaking through his thoughts.

"I'll be there soon!" he replied.

Deep down, he felt absolutely certain that there would be no ghostly manifestation, that some horrific vision of the unfortunately named Maurice Wooden wasn't going to appear seeking vengeance or restitution or peace. He was willing to humor poor old Patricia, however, mainly because he was fascinated by the psychology of people who believed in ghosts. How, he wondered, would Patricia react when no ghost arrived? So far she seemed to be a fairly stable and right-minded woman, but he knew that first impressions could easily be very wrong.

And yet...

And yet, ever since Marlstone Hall, a door in his mind had been left slightly open. Whereas once he would have entirely dismissed any kind of ghost story, now he found himself wondering whether there must just be a chance. That, in truth, was why he'd decided to stick around for an hour or so. If Marlstone Hall had opened his mind to such possibilities, he needed Lotham Lodge to push him back onto the straight and narrow road of logic and reason.

AMY CROSS

CHAPTER EIGHT

THE CAR'S TIRES SCREECHED as Rebecca took a fast right turn off the motorway and onto the road leading to the hospital.

"What's happening back there?" she shouted.

"She's not doing anything!" Alicia sobbed, sitting with Rose's head resting on her lap.

"What do you mean? Is she breathing?"

"I don't know!"

"Check her pulse!"

"I don't know how!"

"Put two fingers on the side of her neck," Rebecca continued breathlessly, half watching the road ahead and half looking back every few seconds. "Just keep searching for some sign that her heart's still beating!"

With tears streaming down her face, Alicia did as she was told. At first she found nothing at all, but after a few seconds she pushed a little harder as she realized that she could just about detect a pulse. A moment later she put the back of her hand against Rose's mouth and nose.

"She's breathing," she stammered. "I mean... I think so. Are we at the hospital yet?"

"Nearly," Rebecca said, and she could see the lights ahead. "Is she still trembling?"

"No."

"What about her mouth? Are there any more bubbles?"

"I don't think so," Alicia replied. "It's like she's not reacting to anything or even hearing our -"

Suddenly Rose's eyes opened wide. Her pupils were huge as she stared up at Alicia's face, but she showed no sign that she actually knew where she was.

"She's awake!" Alicia gasped.

"What do you mean?"

"Her eyes are open but -"

"Tell him!" Rose gurgled, barely able to get any words out as she glared up at Alicia. "Tell him to get out of there!"

"What's she saying?" Rebecca asked, taking a hard turn into the car park outside the hospital's A&E department, causing the tires to complain louder than ever. "I can't make it out!"

"Tell him to get out of there before it comes," Rose continued, tilting her head slightly to one side. "It's really important. Tell him it's not safe to be there, not after the man comes back. The man who shot him is still -"

Before she could finish, her body started shaking violently.

Slamming the brakes on, Rebecca clambered out of the car and immediately started waving at two paramedics who were taking a cigarette break nearby.

"Help us!" she yelled, and already the men were rushing across the car park. "Over here! We've got a young girl who needs help!"

***

"She's sedated now," Doctor Einshorn said, standing with Rebecca in a corridor inside the hospital. "I have to tell you, it took a little longer to work than I expected. Your daughter was very agitated."

"She's not my daughter," Rebecca explained. "She's... we're fostering her. We only just started, actually."

"My best guess at the moment is that she must have experienced some kind of massive epileptic event," he continued. "Are you aware of any history of epilepsy?"

"No," she replied, shaking her head. "I think

they would have told us about something like that, wouldn't they?"

"Absolutely, but you never know when these things can develop. Are you aware of any possible triggers over the past few hours?"

She shook her head.

"I want to keep her in overnight," he continued as he checked some details on his clipboard, "and then we'll ease her out of sedation in the morning. My advice would be for you to go home and try to get some sleep, because there's nothing you can do to help her right now. If you come back at around ten or eleven in the morning, my colleagues will know a lot more and then they can start bringing her around. I'm confident that at that point she should be back to normal, at least for a period of time. Then we can get on with trying to work out what caused all of this in the first place."

"Is there any chance she might be permanently injured?"

"Not that I can see," he said firmly. "It's a good job you got her here so quickly, though. I'll be honest, I've seen cases like this before, but never ones that display quite such intensity. I still have a lot of questions about what happened to Rose tonight, Mrs. Pearson, but those can all wait until she's out of the woods. At the moment our one and only priority has to be getting her through this phase and then easing her out of the other side. The rest can wait. I have to go and check on some other patients, but just try to remain hopeful."

Once the doctor was gone, Rebecca turned and saw Alicia sitting all alone on one of the chairs at the far end of the corridor, just beyond the vending machines.

"Sweetheart, hey," she said as she made her way over. "The doctor thinks she's going to be alright, but we should probably get home for a few hours. Your dad'll be home any minute and I didn't get a chance to leave a note explaining where we are. He's going to be so worried."

"Can't you call him?" she asked as tears continued to fill her eyes.

"I left my phone behind," she said with a sigh.

"What was she talking about?" Alicia continued. "She kept saying that we have to warn someone, that he has to leave somewhere and... and that time's running out. What did she mean by that?"

"I have no idea."

"Was she talking about Daddy?"

"I don't think so," Rebecca replied. "Why would she be? Her mind was probably so scrambled on the way here that she was shouting random things. Besides, your dad really ought to be home round about now. He's probably very worried by the fact that we're not there, so we should get home and tell him what happened before he calls the police."

Alicia thought for a moment, before slowly getting to her feet. As she did so she glanced at the clock on the wall and saw the time.

12.49am.

She wasn't sure that she'd ever been out so late in all her life.

"You did really well tonight," Rebecca said, placing a hand on her daughter's shoulder. "I'm so glad you were with her. If you hadn't been, she might have fallen ill all alone in her bedroom."

"She was -"

Alicia hesitated again, worried about saying too much.

"She was running away," she explained finally. "When I found her, I mean. She was going to run away from us because she thought she was causing us too much trouble. I told her not to go, because I knew you'd be really upset."

"You did a very good job," Rebecca replied, squeezing the girl's shoulder before turning and steering her toward the exit. "I know it's been hard for you, and it's certainly been eventful, but I really think that over time you and Rose are going to become good friends."

"Is she going to die?"

"Of course not."

As they passed an open doorway, Alicia looked into one of the rooms. She immediately froze as she spotted Rose in a bed, surrounded by various machines while wires and other sensors covered her body. For a few seconds the sight was almost too shocking to comprehend, yet Alicia couldn't quite tear her gaze away.

"Do you think she knows what happened?" she asked.

"I really don't have a clue."

"But is she in there?" she continued. "Her mind, I mean. She has to be, doesn't she? If she's not in there, then where else could she be?"

"Now you're asking some pretty deep questions," Rebecca told her. "I'm afraid there's not an expert in the world who can tell you how the human mind really works. We can make educated guesses, but at the end of the day nobody knows for certain. Some people even believe that it's physically impossible for us to ever understand."

"Why?"

"That's... complicated."

Alicia opened her mouth to reply before hesitating for a moment longer. And then, without any warning, she pulled away from her mother and hurried into the room, making her way straight over to the bed and looking down to see Rose's sleeping face.

"I just want to say that I hope you'll get better really soon," she explained, standing on tiptoes in an effort to get a better view of the younger girl's face. "I'm sorry if I haven't been as nice to you as I could have been, I suppose I was just mean because I didn't like the feeling that you were taking so much attention away from me. I shouldn't have been like that and I'm really sorry and I just hope that you can wake up and forgive me."

She waited, hoping that Rose might show some sign that she was starting to stir. When nothing happened, she reached over and gently squeezed her hand.

"Alicia, come on," Rebecca said, watching from the doorway. "She's heavily sedated so there's really no point trying to talk to her right now."

"I know you can hear me," Alicia whispered. "I don't know how, I just know it. Please, whatever's going on in your head, can you just wake up? We just want to have you back here again so that everything can be alright."

CHAPTER NINE

"FIVE MINUTES," PATRICIA SAID, sitting at the dining room table as the wind picked up a little more outside. "It's rather humbling, isn't it? Five minutes from now we shall know, one way or another, whether the ghost of poor Maurice Wooden is really haunting this lodge."

"We certainly will," Jonathan replied from his position opposite her.

"I know you're doubtful," she continued. "The skepticism is positively dripping from your voice. That's the kind of certainty I'm hoping to gain tonight. I would very much like to abandon all superstitions."

"What exactly do you think is supposed to happen?" he asked. "Is some guy with barely any of his head left supposed to just... knock on the door?"

"According to some accounts," she told him. "There are so many different versions of the story. According to one of the most common, Maurice somehow made it back to the lodge under his own steam while the members of the shooting party panicked and tried to work out what they should do next. Eventually one of them followed him and was supposed to finish him off, but he couldn't bring himself to pull the trigger. Or another version says that the poor chap was simply left out there to make his way back to the lodge under his own steam."

"This story keeps changing."

"Like all good stories, I suppose," she mused, before checking her watch. "Four minutes."

"Don't you think there'd be proof by now?" he asked. "If this really happened every year on the same night, at the same time, like clockwork... why wouldn't someone else have come out here to get photos or videos? There would be so many opportunities and the result would be priceless. So... do people just not bother?"

"We'll find out soon enough."

"That's your answer to everything," he pointed out.

"It's one in the morning now. Three minutes to go."

"You know, I really needed this," he added. "Just when there was a danger that I might go getting sentimental, I needed a good kick up the backside. It's nice to be reminded that at the end of the day, I'm just human like everyone else. I've spent the past year wavering in my belief and constantly moving in one direction or another. It's almost as if I caught some kind of fever at Marlstone Hall and I've been trying to shake it ever since. Of course, it'll be a little harder to persuade my wife, but even *she's* not immune to logic."

He pulled his phone out and saw that Rebecca still hadn't responded to his messages.

"I admit that it's a fairly decent spooky story," he said, looking over at Patricia again. "A dead man walking, with his head blasted by some kind of rifle or shotgun. That'd be a very striking image if Mr. Wooden actually showed up tonight, but I don't mind admitting that I won't exactly be holding my breath."

She looked at her watch again.

"Are you going to admit defeat when nothing happens?" he asked.

She kept her gaze on her watch for a few more seconds, before looking up at him.

"Two minutes."

"Or are you going to find excuses?" he continued. "I'll be honest, that would be very disappointing. I'd like to think that once this fantasy deflates like a failed cake in the oven, you'll at least have the decency to acknowledge that the whole thing has been a big waste of time for both of us."

"And will you do the same if it goes the other way?"

"I have a scientific mind."

"That's not an answer."

"It's more of an answer than you could ever imagine," he said, before getting to his feet and stepping into the hallway. Looking at the front door, he saw moonlight filling the glass panel. "There's no sign of anyone so far," he added, unable to avoid a sense of confidence that was now bordering on smugness. "If Maurice Wooden is on his way, shouldn't we know by now? Shouldn't there be the sound of stumbling footsteps? After all, I'd have thought that a man missing most of his head would be pretty unsteady on his feet."

"You're not taking this seriously."

"On the contrary," he replied, turning to her, "I think it's a very important test."

"One minute."

"And why did you leave it until now?" he asked. "You said it yourself, you've worked here for years. So why wait until 2012 to actually come and see what's happening?"

"Fear," she told him through gritted teeth. "Isn't that a good enough reason? Pure, unadulterated fear, Mr. Pearson. I don't mind admitting that even now I'm absolutely terrified. I've tried telling myself that there's no reason to be, but as we get closer and closer to three minutes past one, I can feel all that irrational fear gathering in my chest."

She looked at her watch yet again.

"Thirty seconds," she added.

"In case you're wondering," he replied, "I *will* gloat. Just a little. You can at least allow me that indulgence, can't you? Given the circumstances it'll be a miracle if I don't add a happy little dance too. And to be honest, I'm tired too. Maybe I shouldn't have stayed after all. I've got a long drive ahead."

"Ten seconds."

"This countdown is really starting to get on my -"

"Five seconds."

Leaning back, Jonathan waited for some kind of spooky event. In his head he was counting down from five; he gave a generous few extra seconds at the end, just in case the ghostly figure of Maurice Wooden might have been delayed, but already he could see the disappointment in Patricia's eyes. He watched as she looked at the window, and for a moment they both listened to the sound of wind battering the building. Although he wasn't entirely sure when he should break the silence, Jonathan knew full well that sooner rather than later he was going to have to declare victory and get back to his car.

Finally Patricia opened her mouth, as if she was about to say something, but at the last second she held back.

"I'm sorry," Jonathan told her.

She watched the window for a moment longer before turning to him.

"For what it's worth," he continued, "I derive no pleasure from watching someone fail to get what they want. I know you wanted a ghost to show up, so I'm sorry that nothing happened."

Again he waited, but Patricia seemed unwilling to break her own silence, as if she was somehow still clinging to the hope that something might occur.

"Do you need me to drive you anywhere?" Jonathan asked, getting to his feet, causing the chair's legs to scrape against the floor in the process.

"I... think we should give it a few more minutes," she said softly.

"You said it was due to happen at precisely three minutes past one in the morning," he reminded her.

"Yes, but -"

Falling silent again, she seemed lost for words.

"Do you think he's just running late?" he asked. "Do you think he got distracted by something? Or he just set off a few minutes after he should have? I thought that in most of these spooky stories the dead were supposed to be pretty reliable."

"I'm terribly sorry," she said after a moment, slowly getting up. "You must think that I'm a frightfully silly old woman."

"I didn't say that."

"But you're thinking it, aren't you?" she continued. "You must be. I certainly am. I admit, I was rather sure that *something* was going to happen. I wasn't even sure what that something would be, but I barely acknowledged the possibility that there might simply be nothing at all."

"There's nothing wrong with hoping for a little mystery in the world," he suggested. "Listen, this has been an interesting little diversion but it's really getting late now and I've still got a way to drive. I'd be happy to drop you off something along the way, though."

"Such a fool," she muttered under her breath, while shaking her head as if she couldn't quite believe the outcome of her little experiment.

"Mrs. Windermere?" Jonathan said, a little more firmly this time. "I'd feel bad leaving you out here all alone. Where exactly do you live?"

"You're quite right," she replied, as if she'd just woken from some kind of reverie. "Would you mind... would you mind giving me a moment or two to gather my thoughts? Once I've done that, I should be very grateful for a lift into the village. It's only a very short drive away and it looked to me as if you were going that way anyway."

"I'll be outside," he told her, before stepping back. "Again, I'm sorry. I wish tonight could have worked out better for you."

As he sauntered out of the room, Jonathan was already starting to think that his visit to Lotham Lodge had been an unusual little diversion – but one that, all things considered, served as a neat little coda to his entire flirtation with the paranormal. If he'd needed something to top and tail the whole experience, and to put a ribbon on the return of his absolute skepticism, then this particular encounter had done the job. And as he headed toward the front door, he figured that the incident only confirmed that he'd been right to omit the final section of the presentation.

Explaining that to Rebecca, however, might be more difficult.

And then, as he reached for the handle of the front door, he spotted movement out of the corner of his eye. Turning, he looked through into the old kitchen and saw the table bathed in moonlight, and for a moment – just a brief fraction of a second – he felt as if he'd spotted someone in there. He knew that Patricia was in the dining room and that there was no other way into the kitchen, so after a few seconds he walked cautiously to the door and peered through.

He waited, but he saw no sign of anyone. Still, feeling that his curiosity had been piqued, he stepped into the room so that he could look around properly. Leaning down, he looked under the table, but so far there was no obvious place where anyone could hide. Standing up straight again, he saw the empty hooks on the opposite wall, and already he was starting to figure that he must have simply imagined things.

"If Rebecca could see me now," he said with a sigh as he rubbed the back of his head, "she'd never let me drive. She'd tell me to -"

Before he could get another word out, the door creaked loudly as it swung shut with a gentle bump. Turning, Jonathan made his way over and grabbed the handle, only to find this time that it was somehow locked.

"Hello?" he called out, knocking on the wood in the hope that Patricia would come to his rescue. "Mrs. Windermere? I'm not sure what's going on, but I seem to be trapped in here. Would you mind -"

Suddenly he heard a distinct and very low cracking sound coming from behind his shoulder, as if something was very slowly unfolding in the darkness.

AMY CROSS

CHAPTER TEN

"ARE WE GOING HOME now?" Alicia asked, once she'd finally become slightly bored sitting in the back of the motionless car. "Mummy?"

"Just give me a minute," Rebecca replied, staring out across the car park and watching the lights of the hospital. "I don't know, I'm probably being paranoid but I can't help thinking..."

Her voice trailed off for a few seconds.

"Rose is going to be okay, isn't she?" Alicia added. "You told me she would be. You said the doctor promised."

"Doctors don't really make a lot of promises," Rebecca explained, turning to her, "but he was certainly hopeful. I think it's just the idea of leaving her behind that's worrying me. What if she wakes up in the middle of the night and there's no-one with her?"

"Didn't the doctor say she was going to sleep all night?"

Rebecca hesitated, before nodding slowly.

"You look really tired," Alicia told her.

"Thank you."

"You've got bags under your eyes."

"Thank you again."

"You've got wrinkles and -"

"Thank you, Alicia," Rebecca said, a little more firmly this time – although she was too tired to actually feel offended in any way. "And I know you're right. Rose has no idea what's going on at the moment and it'll be better for her if we're fit and rested in the morning. I just hate the idea of abandoning her here with a bunch of strangers. She's already been abandoned so many times before."

"We can stay if you want," Alicia told her.

"No, we need to go," Rebecca said finally, turning and starting the engine, then backing the car out of its parking spot. "You're right, Rose is going to sleep all night and we just need to make sure that we're there for her in the morning. Let's get home and try to rest."

As the car rumbled toward the car park's exit, Alicia turned and looked back at the hospital. Thinking about Rose in the bed, with so many wires and tubes all around her, she couldn't help but wish that she'd been nicer to the new arrival. In that moment she told herself that, if Rose ever woke up again, she was going to do whatever she could to become her new best friend.

***

"Just keep checking according to the usual rota," Doctor Einshorn said as he stood at a desk on the hospital ward. "I don't anticipate you having any dramas during the night, but you know the procedure to follow in case anything happens."

"What about the little girl in room six?" Henry asked. "She's sedated, right?"

"There's not much chance of her waking up tonight," Einshorn said as they both turned to look through a nearby open doorway.

Rose was still on the bed, still unconscious and attached to various machines.

"Harrison can take over in the morning," Einshorn added, setting his clipboard down before turning and walking away. "If you need anything, page him, not me. I've got a big golf game tomorrow afternoon so I need my beauty sleep. Ever since I got into this hickory stuff I've been playing so much better."

"Sure thing," Henry muttered as he grabbed the clipboard and quickly familiarized himself with the details. "Asshole."

Once he was sure he knew what he was doing, he turned to head to the office, only to stop as he looked into room six again and suddenly saw that Rose was sitting up. Not only was she bolt upright in the bed, with the wires and tubes hanging down from her body, she was also staring directly at him.

"Hey," he said, making his way over to the doorway. "You're not supposed to be..."

His voice trailed off, and then he turned and looked along the corridor.

"Doctor Einshorn?" he called out, even though he knew he was already too late.

He waited, and then he turned to look into the room, only to let out a startled gasp as he saw that Rose was now out of the bed. All the wires and tubes were still connecting her to the machines, but she was standing barefoot on the linoleum floor as she stared at Henry with a strangely calm expression on her face.

"You're not supposed to be up," he told her. "At least... I don't think you are."

"Someone has to get him out of there," she replied.

"I'm sorry?"

"I tried to warn them before," she continued. "Someone has to get him out of there. It's too late to stop him going in, but he's trapped now. He has to get out before they wake up properly."

"You're... being creepy right now," Henry replied, stepping cautiously into the room. "Listen, you need to get back into bed and then I'll call whoever's on duty."

Looking at one of the tubes, he saw that a strong sedative was still hooked up to the girl's arm. Assuming that the sedative was still being delivered into her system, there was no way she should be awake.

"There isn't much time," she told him.

"Yeah, you keep saying cryptic stuff like that," he replied, before reaching down and taking her hand. "If -"

Before he could stop himself, he instantly recoiled. Rose's skin was so icy that even touching her was almost painful. Already Henry could see that she was becoming paler and paler, and he was starting to think that he simply needed to call for someone who had a better idea what was happening.

"Can you get back into bed for me?" he asked.

"Why aren't you doing something to help him?"

"You're really not making a whole lot of sense," he replied. "I'm not your actual doctor, I don't know too much about whatever's wrong with you. I can go and get one of the other nurses, though, and she can decide whether to call a doctor."

He waited, but the girl was still staring at him.

"Can you wait right here?" he continued finally. "Do you think you can do that?"

"No-one's listening to me."

"I need to find someone who can decide whether to -"

"He won't make it out of there," she said firmly, clenching her fists now as if she was slowly becoming overwhelmed by anger. "He doesn't understand how much danger he's in. He's going to turn his back on them, or he's not going to believe that they're real, or he's going to do something else that's going to get him -"

She fell silent for a moment as she began to furrow her brow, and after a few seconds a tear began to run down her left cheek.

"They're going to kill him," she added, and now her voice was trembling. "You have to listen to me, if you don't... they're going to kill him. You have to tell Mrs. Pearson to go and get him out of there. But it's too late, she's not close enough, that means there's no-one who can save him."

"Little girl," Henry said holding up both hands, "you're not making any -"

"Someone has to save him!" she shouted, stumbling forward – only for the wires and tubes to hold her back. Clearly confused, she began to try pulling them away, causing alarms to sound on several of the machines.

"Don't do that!" Henry said, hurrying toward her and trying to hold her still. "Leave -"

"Get off me!" she screamed, biting his forearm hard and immediately drawing blood.

Letting out a gasp of pain, Henry tried desperately to pull away but already Rose had managed to pull one of the monitors away from the wall. As the screen crashed down and smashed against the floor, the girl twisted first one way and then the other as she let go of the his arm and tried again to run out of the room. Before she could manage more than a couple of paces, however, she jerked back and slammed against the side of the bed. As she hit the floor, she was already shaking violently again as if her entire body was filled with a powerful hidden force that was slowly trying to force its way out.

"What's going on in here?" one of the nurses yelled as she rushed through, only to immediately drop to her knees next to Rose. "We need a full team in here!" she shouted, turning to Henry. "Now!"

As Henry stumbled out of the room, the nurse turned Rose over and looked down into her eyes. Saliva was bubbling on the girl's lips and her body was shaking harder than ever, but she was still somehow trying to get some words out.

"Save him!" she gurgled, rolling her eyes back in their sockets just as two more nurses hurried into the room to help. "He doesn't know how much danger he's in! You have to get him out of there before it's too late!"

CHAPTER ELEVEN

TURNING, JONATHAN LOOKED BACK across the darkened kitchen. He still saw nothing other than the bare table, with moonlight streaming through a window at the far end of the room, but the cracking sound continued for several seconds before finally falling silent again.

"Hello?" he said cautiously, taking a step forward. "Is anyone in here?"

He stopped to look around, but a moment later he realized that he could now hear the faintest rattling sound. At first he had no idea where this sound was coming from, until he happened to glance at the hooks on the wall. Making his way over, he saw that several of these metal hooks were shaking slightly, as if they were trying to break away from the wall.

Puzzled as to what force could possibly be causing this phenomenon, Jonathan slowly reached up and touched one of the hooks, and he immediately found that it felt unusually cold. A moment later he heard a brief splitting sound, and he turned to see that one of the other hooks further along the row had begun to come away from the wall.

"Mrs. Windermere?" he called out, glancing over at the door again. "There's not... I don't know, there's not a train line running near here, is there? Or a history of earthquakes?"

He waited for an answer, but the hooks were still rattling – although this time none of the rest seemed to be threatening to burst free from the wall.

"Mrs. Windermere, can you let me out of here, please?" he asked, making his way back to the door and grabbing the handle, only to find that it was still locked. "Mrs. Windermere, I don't know if this is your idea of some kind of joke, but I don't appreciate being held captive."

He gave the handle several more tries before giving up and banging on the door instead. When even that failed to elicit an answer, he instead flicked the switch on the wall, hoping to at least bring some light to proceedings. The bulb above failed to respond, even as the rattling sound became more extreme.

After glancing over his shoulder and seeing

that the hooks were still shaking, he banged on the door once more.

"Mrs. Windermere," he continued, "I'm going to have to insist that you let me out of here right now. I've got a mobile phone with me and I'm not afraid to use it. If I have to, if you give me no choice, I'll have no hesitation in calling the police."

He waited, before pulling his phone out.

"I'm holding it now," he added, hoping to call the old woman's bluff as he typed 999. "I've put the number in, now all that's left is for me to press one last button and call. Is that what you want? Do you want police cars racing out here to Lotham Lodge in the middle of the night? How do you think your employer would react to the news that you're wandering around like this?"

Again he waited, but he was starting to realize that perhaps he was going to have to go through with his threat. He had no idea exactly how he was going to explain the situation, yet he figured that he couldn't simply stay in the kitchen for the rest of the night. At the same time, he could already see that his phone had no bars, so any attempt to call the police would have to wait.

A moment later, coming up with another idea, he marched around the table and headed to the window, only to find that this too was stubbornly locked.

The hooks, meanwhile, had at least stopped

rattling.

"Okay, Mrs. Windermere!" he called out loudly, determined to make sure that she'd be able to hear him from anywhere in the house. "I'm not joking, I really will -"

In that moment he froze as he saw a dozen or so deer carcasses hanging from the hooks. Some of the dead animals had been skinned ready for butchering, while others still had their fur and even their heads. Astonished by the sight and convinced that they couldn't have simply arrived in the blink of an eye, he stared at them for several seconds as he tried to wrap his mind around this latest development. And then, slowly stepping closer, he reached out and placed a hand against one of the skinned corpses, quickly finding that its meat was firm but cold to the touch.

And real.

Very real.

"What the..."

He knew that the dead animals hadn't been there a moment earlier, but he also knew that there was no way that anyone could have introduced them to the room in the blink of an eye. That only left, he realized quickly, some kind of revolving door that must have swung around in the exact moment when he wasn't looking. Sure, the idea was impractical and almost impossible to believe, but he was struggling to come up with any other explanation.

Making his way along the wall, he began to search for some hint of the mechanism, although he soon had to admit that it was well hidden. Reaching the far end, he looked at one of the skinned deer and saw that it still had its hooves and head, albeit with all the skin and fur having long since been removed. The belly, meanwhile, had been carved open to reveal a cavity, no doubt marking the spot where the organs had at some point been removed.

"Is this supposed to scare me?" he shouted. "Mrs. Windermere, I must admit that you have a wonderful gift for macabre theatricality but this is really neither the time nor the place. It's well beyond one in the morning and I really must insist that you let me go. If you don't, I'll..."

He wondered for a moment how to complete that threat, before looking at a nearby chair and then turning his attention to the window. As much as he hated the idea of smashing a window and forcing his way out of the house, he was starting to realize that he might not have many other options, so after a few seconds he stepped closer to the chair and picked it up. The idea of smashing a window in any property – and especially one that was clearly so old and full of historical value – horrified him, and he had no wish to be a vandal, but at the same time he felt that he had no choice.

Standing on front of the window, he held the chair up and prepared to strike, but a moment later he realized that he could hear the strange rattling sound once more.

Turning, he saw that several of the deer carcasses were now twitching slightly on the hooks. His first thought was that the hooks themselves were causing this to happen, but after a few seconds he began to realize that the opposite seemed to be the case: it appeared that the carcasses were the ones creating the movement, and that the hooks were merely reacting.

Slowly lowering the chair, he set it on the table before stepping over to the dead animals. Sure enough, he saw that not only were they twitching but in some cases their muscles seemed to be shaking almost as if they were suffering from some kind of seizure. Astonished by the idea that dead meat could react in such a way, he reached out and touched one of the corpses, and he quickly realized that the muscles and tendons themselves were apparently reacting to some kind of stimulus.

Reaching up, he gently touched the back of his hand against the side of a hook, but he felt no kind of electric charge. So much, he realized immediately, for that idea.

Stepping back, he told himself that he really didn't need to resolve this particular mystery, not at well past one in the morning. He turned to go back over to the chair, but at that moment one of the carcasses seemingly jumped from the hook and landed with a heavy, slightly dusty thud on the floor. A fraction of a second later another carcass fell, then another, and Jonathan backed away around the table as he saw that most of them were now down, although a few were still caught on the hooks.

"Mrs. Windermere," he said out loud, convinced that the woman must be lurking on the other side of the door and that she was most likely enjoying his discomfort. "I don't quite know what you think you're going to achieve with this bizarre little display, but let me assure you that I'm immune to such... theatricality."

He waited, listening out for any hint of laughter, and then he turned and headed once more to the window.

"When Rebecca hears about this," he said under his breath, "she'll -"

Before he could finish, he heard a low rumbling sound, a kind of slow-birthing cry that began to twist in the air until it resembled a stuttering shriek.

He froze for a moment, with one hand on the chair, before turning to look back at the row of hooks. He could see that most of them were motionless now, although the ones still holding up deer carcasses were rattling, but the shriek seemed to be coming from the floor. The table was in the way, blocking his view of the fallen corpses, yet after a few seconds he heard another groan, as if something was being born into the world. The sound seemed almost unreal, like something filled with agony, and then – just as he'd begun to convince himself that he was imagining things – the table suddenly shuddered as if it had been hit by something heavy.

He instinctively took a step back.

"Mrs. Windermere, I need you to let me out of this room immediately," he said, and now he was unable to hide the fear in his voice. "If you don't, I'll go to the police and press charges for false imprisonment."

Swallowing hard, he waited for her to respond, but a moment later he spotted something moving in the darkness. To his horror, he could only stare as one of the bloodied and skinned deer carcasses slowly rose up – and a fleshy head turned toward him and let out a gasping, guttural scream.

CHAPTER TWELVE

"OKAY," JONATHAN SAID, BACKING away slowly and holding up his hands as he saw that two more of the creatures were also stumbling unsteadily to their feet on the other side of the table. "I don't know what's going on here, but -"

In that moment one of the deer screamed again, but this time its cry was much louder than before. Lifting its head up, the tattered animal looked toward the window as scraps of pinky-red meat hung from exposed sections of its skull. A milky white eye twitched and flickered in the exposed socket, and a moment later another of the deer lurched forward and hit the table again, this time with more force than before. The animals all appeared to be lost and out of control, as if they had no idea how or why they'd suddenly been dragged kicking and screaming back into the world.

"Mrs. Windermere," Jonathan continued, struggling now to keep from panicking, "I don't know what this freak show is all about but I insist that you stop it at once. These... these puppets are obscene!"

As those words left his lips, he told himself that indeed this must be what he was seeing: somehow someone, most likely engaged for that very task by Patricia Windermere, had succeeded in animating the corpses of a dozen deer. Although he was no expert on such things, he felt sure that some highly ingenious tech expert would be able to drill animatronics into the dead animals' bones, forcing them to mimic some semblance of life itself. Sure, in broad daylight the effect would probably be rather poor, but at night in a moonlit room the entire scene conjured up an ethereal and almost unearthly sight.

Hurrying to the door, he tried the light switch again, still to no avail.

Behind him, another of the dead deer slipped and fell back down, crying out as it did so and then immediately trying again to haul itself up.

"Mrs. Windermere, enough is enough!" Jonathan shouted, pounding on the door with all the force he could muster. "I won't tell you again! This is false imprisonment and... and deception, and I'm not going to stand for it! Let me out of here at once!"

He gave her a fraction of a second to respond before slamming his fist against the door and then turning to grab the chair. Before he had a chance, however, two of the deer fell against the table and knocked it across the room, sending it slamming against the opposite wall with such force that the chair toppled over and fell to the floor. The deer seemed to be panicking now, and Jonathan felt as if they were acting almost as if they were only now being born into the world.

Reaching into his pocket, he was shocked to see that his hands were trembling as he pulled his phone out. The screen still showed no signal but he figured that he had to try; he knew he had to call the police, but he actually found it somewhat difficult to hit the 9 button three times and -

Suddenly one of the deer screamed and lurched at him, slamming into his side and knocking him off balance. Almost falling, he managed to steady himself at the last second but the phone fell from his hands and was immediately kicked away by the deer's frantic hooves as the animal struggled desperately to remain upright.

Reaching down, Jonathan tried to reach for the phone, but in that moment the deer cried out again, this time blasting his face with cold, rancid air. Pulling back, he could only stare in horror as the animal tilted its head to one side, in the process tearing some of the flesh on the side of its own neck.

"Mr. Pearson?" Patricia called out suddenly from the other side of the door. "Are you in there? Whatever's causing that dreadful noise?"

"Unlock the door!" he shouted.

He saw the handle twitching, followed by a series of thuds, yet the door still refused to open.

"It seems to be locked," she told him. "Do you have a key in there?"

"Of course I don't have a key!" he yelled angrily, trying to slip past the deer even as two more stumbled toward him, backing him once again into the corner. "It's your bloody house! Get that door open right now!"

"What are those awful sounds?" she stammered.

"Get these things away from me!" he spluttered, ducking down and finally slipping past three of the animals, rushing to the chair and hauling it up. "I won't be held responsible for any damage!"

This time he didn't hesitate. Throwing the chair, he smashed one of the window panes and then immediately set about breaking the rest while also trying to destroy the horizontal and vertical wooden mullions holding them together. Finding that the old wood was tougher than he'd expected, he had to slam the chair repeatedly against the mullions and struggled to slowly break them apart.

"Mr. Pearson, open this door at once!" Patricia shouted, still banging on the door. "What are you doing in there? This is an old house and -"

At that moment one of the deer let out an even louder and shriller cry than before as it somehow haphazardly stumbled up onto the table.

"What was that noise?" Patricia gasped. "What -"

Crying out again, the deer – in a state of panic – stumbled along the table. Knocking Jonathan out of the way, the dead animal launched itself at the window in a desperate attempt to break out of the room. Unable to force its way through, however, the creature merely slammed into the broken pieces of wood and shards of glass, quickly becoming trapped as it tried frantically and in vain to break free.

Still holding the chair, Jonathan could only step back and watch the moonlit horror as the dead deer proceeded to rip its own body apart against what remained of the window. Desperately pulling in every direction as it attempted to get outside, the animal appeared to not understand that in the process it was only forcing the broken glass deeper into its body, while the splintered wooden ends of the mullions were embedding themselves into its flesh and holding it tightly in place, almost crucifying it in several parts of its body at once.

Turning its head slightly, the deer cried out once more, but this time one of the wooden ends was rupturing the side of its neck, gouging out dead meat.

"This can't be happening," Jonathan stammered, refusing to believe that he was witnessing anything other than some kind of extremely effective but complex trick.

"Open this door at once!" Patricia shouted, trying the handle yet again. "Mr. Pearson, if you don't open up immediately I shall be forced to call the police! Do you understand?"

Looking around, Jonathan spotted his phone on the floor. He rushed over as the animal trapped in the window continued to scream, but as he picked the phone up he immediately saw that one of the hooves had shattered the screen. A moment later he heard another cry, and he turned just in time to see that a second deer was now also trying to break out through the window, although this animal was only succeeding in forcing the wood and glass deeper and deeper into the corpse of its predecessor.

"I have to get out of here," Jonathan told himself, before starting to make his way back around the table, heading to the door. All he knew in that moment was that -

Suddenly another deer crashed into him, briefly crushing him against the wall. He turned and tried to get away, but the deer was also attempting to escape and – in the process – the animal kicked out hard, slamming a sharp hoof straight into Jonathan's ribs with such force that he could only let out a gasp as an excruciatingly sharp pain burst through one side of his body.

Struggling to breathe, he slid town onto the floor as the deer rushed to the other end of the room. Unable to get to the window, the animal turned and stumbled back, hitting the table and crying out again. Meanwhile the other dead deer were also screaming and groaning, filling the room with a cacophony of hideously unreal calls as Jonathan immediately tried to haul himself up.

Wincing, he felt another sharp pain in his side, cutting up through his rib cage. Coughing, he felt yet more pain, this time a little higher up, and he realized after a moment that he could taste blood at the back of his throat. He had to lean against the wall for a little support, and already he worried that he was getting short of breath. After taking a moment to try to pull himself together, he looked over at the door and told himself that his only hope now was to somehow find a way to break through.

"Mr. Pearson, are you okay in there?" Patricia shouted, still banging on the door's other side. "Mr. Pearson -"

"Stand back!" he shouted at the top of his voice. "I'm going to break it down!"

"What do you -"

"Get out of the way!" he yelled. "I'm going to... I have to..."

He took a moment to try to summon every last ounce of strength in his body, before rushing toward the door with his right shoulder. The deer were screaming all around him, but at the last second one of the animals lurched into his way and slammed straight into him, hitting his head with its skull and knocked him out cold. With one last gasp of pain, Jonathan slumped down against the floor and was already unconscious by the time his head hit the wooden boards.

CHAPTER THIRTEEN

A KEY CLICKED AND scratched briefly in the lock, before turning and finally allowing the door to swing open. The hinges creaked slightly, breaking the otherwise all-consuming silence.

"Okay, we're home," Rebecca said, setting her keys in the bowl on the hallway table and then switching the lights on before turning to usher Alicia into the house. "It's straight up to bed for you, young lady."

"Where's Daddy?" the young girl asked, stepping over to the foot of the stairs. "His car wasn't outside."

"It must be in the garage," Rebecca replied, pushing the door shut and then looking over at the shoe rack.

Glancing around the hallway, she realized

that in fact there was no sign of Jonathan at all. She knew he should have been home already, yet there wasn't even the slightest hint of the usual mess he made whenever he returned from a trip. Turning to look at the bowl again, she realized that hers were the only keys.

"Jonathan?" she called out, still convinced that he had to be around somewhere.

"Where is he?" Alicia asked.

"He's fine," Rebecca said, trying to hide her concern as she took her daughter by the hand and forced her to start climbing the stairs. "Listen, I need you to brush your teeth for me and go straight to bed, okay? I'll be up to check on you very soon, but by then I want you to be all tucked up. Can you do that for me?"

Alicia thought for a moment before nodding. She began to make her way up, and then she stopped and looked back down.

"Mummy," she said cautiously, "do you think any of this is my fault?"

"What are you talking about?" Rebecca asked, unable to hide a sense of genuine exhaustion.

"Just that... I could have been nicer to Rose and now she's poorly. What if that's because of me?"

"Of course it isn't," Rebecca said, forcing a smile. "Now go to bed, okay? We've got to be up early to go back to the hospital and check on her."

Once Alicia had made her way upstairs, Rebecca headed through to the kitchen. Still seeing no sign of her husband, she grabbed her phone and immediately saw several missed calls.

"Where are you?" she muttered under her breath as she pressed the button to call him back.

She held the phone up to the side of her face and waited for him to answer, but she was immediately put through to his voicemail. Sighing, she checked her own voicemail and realized that she had a couple of messages.

"Hey," she heard his voice saying as she played the first message, "so this is going to sound strange but I'm taking a brief detour on the way home to a place called Lotham Lodge. It sounds like it'd be right up your alley, actually. There's this woman who claims that it's haunted and... I mean, the whole thing has kind of dropped into my lap in some ways, so I figure I might as well give it a look. I'll probably be an hour or two later home. Don't wait up too long."

Once that message was over, she furrowed her brow as she brought up the second.

"Me again," Jonathan's voice said. "Not much to report, but it's taking a little longer than I planned. You've probably gone to bed by now. I just wanted to let you know that I'll be a few hours later. Everything's okay, it's just that I've found myself in a somewhat improbable situation and..."

He fell silent for a moment.

"I'll tell you all about it when I get back," he continued. "I think you'll probably be rather enamored of the whole story once you hear the details. Just don't wait up, okay? I hope you and the girls have had a nice evening. I can't wait to join you and -"

In that moment the message ended.

"Where the hell are you?" she muttered, trying again to call him but still only getting through to his voicemail. She hesitated, before deciding that she needed to leave a message. "Jonathan," she said firmly, "call me when you get this. It's important. You have to get home as fast as you can, I... I need you, Jonathan. It's about Rose. Something really strange is happening with Rose."

***

"I need you, Jonathan," Rebecca's voice continued, drifting up from the kitchen downstairs. "It's about Rose. Something really strange is happening with Rose."

Kneeling on the landing, hiding in the shadows as she peered between the railings, Alicia watched the hallway below. She knew she should be brushing her teeth by now and that she really shouldn't do anything that might cause her mother more stress, but at the same time she was wide awake and all sorts of thoughts were swirling through her thoughts. Unable to shake the feeling that she was somehow responsible for everything that was happening to Rose, she also knew there was nothing she could do in that moment to put it all right, yet...

Yet somehow that sense of powerlessness was eating away at her.

Suddenly hearing her mother's footsteps, she braced herself to pull back. Instead she spotted Rebecca walking though into the living room.

Getting to her feet, Alicia briefly considered going back downstairs and trying to talk to her mother, but she knew there was no real point. She was used to being thought of as too young to understand anything, to being shut out of any important discussions; she'd barely even been consulted about the idea of letting Rose move in, a decision that she felt should have been discussed a little more beforehand. And as she turned and traipsed through to her bedroom, she realized that it wasn't Rose she'd been against exactly, it was more the fact that nobody had listened to her opinions about the matter.

Nobody had even asked.

Once she was in her room, she left the lights off as she walked over to her bed. She still wasn't remotely tired, not in the slightest, but when she looked at her alarm clock she saw that the time was already well past one in the morning and she wasn't sure she'd ever been up so late.

"Rose," she whispered, even though she knew she was probably being foolish, "you can't hear me, but... if you can somehow, please be okay. I'll never be mean to you again, just... please wake up."

As she stood in silence, waiting for some kind of answer, she began to wonder whether she was praying. She wasn't even quite sure what it meant to pray, but as the seconds passed she told herself that there was no real harm in at least trying. And as much as she knew that her parents probably wouldn't approve, she figured that she was willing to do whatever it took to try to help Rose.

After looking over her shoulder to make sure that there was no chance of her mother walking in, she quickly dropped to her knees and put her hands together in front of her face.

"God," she continued, lowering her voice even more, "I don't even know if you're real, but if you are, can you please help Rose? I don't know what's wrong with her but I think she's in trouble, and I think... I think it might be too much trouble for Mummy and Daddy and the doctors to deal with on their own. Can you please -"

Suddenly something sharp hit her left cheek.

Letting out a gasp, she pulled away and fell down against the floor just as something rattled down onto the wooden floorboards nearby.

Startled, she sat in silence for a moment before reaching up and touching her cheek. Feeling a slight cut, she held her finger out and spotted a trace of blood. She had no idea what could have hit her, but after a few seconds she reached out and switched on the bedside lamp, and the first thing she saw was her farmyard play collection on the table, with lots of little plastic toy animals dotted around.

Struggling to stop herself crying, she looked around the room and saw something on the floor nearby. Crawling over, she picked the object up and turned it over, and she was surprised to see that one of the toy deer from the table appeared to have flown across the room of its own volition. She touched one of the hooves and felt the sharp edge, and she quickly realized that this must have been the object that had hit her.

Getting to her feet, she walked over to the desk and looked at her own reflection in the mirror. She saw the faintest dribble of blood on her cheek, and then she looked down at the toy deer and saw that a tiny speck of blood had been left on the plastic.

A moment later, hearing footsteps on the stairs, she set the deer down and raced to the bed, quickly diving under the covers and turning the lamp off. Although she wanted to tell her mother about the small cut on her cheek, she was also keen to avoid causing trouble and she figured that the injury was only teeny tiny. As she heard her door creaking open, she rolled over onto her side and tried to bury her face under the sheet.

She waited, and a few seconds later the door bumped shut again.

Rolling onto her back, Alicia stared up at the ceiling and felt that for the first time in her life she'd actually been grown up about something. Ordinarily she would have run to her mother and cried about the scratch on her cheek, but this time she'd managed to hold herself together. Still, as she looked across the room and saw the farmyard toys once again, she couldn't help but wonder how some stray gust of wind could have thrown the deer so hard and so fast.

CHAPTER FOURTEEN

"MR. PEARSON, CAN YOU hear me? Mr. Pearson, please wake up. Say something. What on -"

Suddenly opening his eyes, Jonathan saw Patricia Windermere leaning over him with a terribly anxious expression on her face.

"Mr. Pearson, are you okay?" she continued. "What in the name of all that's holy went on in here? What happened to you?"

For a few seconds, Jonathan had absolutely no idea how to answer that question. He had a vague memory of having turned up at Lotham Lodge on some hare-brained mission to investigate a possible ghost, and he remembered sitting at a table with Patricia, but a few more seconds passed before the rest of the night's events began to slowly reassemble in his mind. He thought back to the failure of the ghostly Maurice Wooden to arrive, and to his rather difficult attempt to keep from seeming too smug about the result, and then...

And then he remembered the dead deer.

"What the -"

Startled, he sat up so fast that he almost headbutted Patricia as she just about managed to pull out of the way in time.

Looking around the old kitchen, he saw now that there was no sign of the animals. A large section of the window at the far end of the room was broken, but there were no deer wedged into the smashed wood and glass; the table had been pushed aside but there was nothing to indicate the cause, while the metal hooks remained innocently in place along the entire extent of the opposite wall. Moonlight was still shining through the stained glass section of the window.

"I heard the most tremendous crashing sounds coming from in here," Patricia said, "and something else, like... I don't know how to explain it, but it sounded like quite terrible screams or... or cries. Was it you making those awful noises, Mr. Pearson?"

He turned to her.

"You look utterly dreadful," she continued. "I almost fetched the police and the ambulance folk, and now I'm starting to think that I should have."

"I'm fine," he replied as he tried to get up. "I'm just -"

Suddenly he let out a gasp of pain and slumped back down as he felt a burst of agony ripping up through the right hand side of his ribs. Shocked, he winced as he tried to shift his weight in an increasingly desperate attempt to ease the pain a little, but he was already absolutely certain that something must be very wrong. He remembered the deer hoof slamming into his body, and the crash against another deer that had knocked him out, and he could only manage a faint groan as he tried once more to understand exactly what had happened.

"*Should* I fetch an ambulance?" Patricia asked.

"What time is it?" he replied, and he was disturbed to realize that even talking was slightly painful now.

He felt sure that – at the very least – he must have fractured a rib or two.

"It's a little before quarter to two."

"Quarter to..."

Shocked, he reached into his pocket for his phone, before spotting it smashed on the floor nearby.

"Rebecca's going to start worrying," he stammered. "Hopefully she's asleep, but at some point she's going to wake up and realize that something's wrong."

"Is Rebecca your wife?"

"I have to get home," he said. "I'm sorry, but do you mind helping me up?"

"I'm not sure that you're in any condition to drive," she pointed out.

"I didn't ask for your opinion on -"

Stopping himself just in time, he reminded himself that there was no point allowing his anger to take control.

"Can you *please* just help me up?" he asked after a moment. "I know I'm injured but I'm fairly sure that I can make it home, and then first thing after I get some rest I'll drag my sorry ass to a hospital. Just help me get to my car and everything'll be alright."

"If you insist," she mumbled, doing her best to support him. "Are you ready?"

He took a deep breath before starting again to get up from the floor. After just a couple of seconds, however, he let out an agonized cry as he felt broken ribs slicing against one another inside his chest. Although he tried for a few more seconds to push through the pain, he'd already broken out into a cold sweat and finally he had no choice other than to admit defeat. Capitulating, he lowered himself back down and leaned against the wall as he tried to find the strength from somewhere to make another attempt.

"You can't even stand," Patricia observed.

"Just give me a minute."

"There's really no way around it," she continued. "I shall have to go and get some help. And seeing as your mobile telephone has been damaged, it would seem that my only option is to drive to the village."

He started shaking his head.

"There isn't another choice, Mr. Pearson," she said firmly.

"Why about *your* phone?"

"Mine?" she scoffed. "I don't have one of those wretched things! The idea of people being able to get hold of me at any time of the day or night is just intolerable. And before you ask, there's no telephone here, either. Lotham Lodge is more or less abandoned these days, so the only way to get help is for someone to go to the village. And in case it has escaped your attention, you're in no fit state to travel. You can't even get to the car."

"Help me," he said through gritted teeth, trying to deny the pain. "I can do it."

"Piffle," she insisted. "Mr. Pearson, I have to admit that I'm getting on in years. I can't support you, not when you're in such a dreadful state."

She held her hand out toward him.

"You shall have to give me your keys."

"Are you insane?"

"Or would you rather wait here for a passerby?" she asked, raising a skeptical eyebrow.

"Let me assure you that we'll both be waiting a very long time. There isn't exactly a lot of traffic in this neck of the woods."

He opened his mouth to argue with her, but deep down he was starting to worry that she might be right. He looked over once more at his wrecked phone, and then he looked at Patricia as he tried to think of some other plan, and then slowly he pulled his keys out and deposited them with a hint of anger in her hand. He was still very far from convinced that this was a good idea.

"It's an automatic," he murmured.

"A what?"

"The gears. It's an automatic."

"Righty-ho," she said, getting to her feet. "I really shouldn't be too long. You'll be okay here without me, won't you?"

She waited for an answer.

"Mr. Pearson -"

"Of course I'll be okay here without you," he spat back at her, fully aware that the pain in his ribs was making him more short-tempered than usual... but unable to help himself. "What exactly do you think might cause me problems?"

"Well... whatever did this to you, I suppose," she replied, staring at him with a somewhat pitying expression.

"There was a loose deer in here," he muttered. "Two or three, actually. It was dark, I couldn't really see what was going on." He hesitated, before looking up at the ceiling – where a bulb was burning bright. "There's power in here?"

"Yes, we have these things called lights switches," she told him with an air of disdain. "You were in the dark when I found you. Why did you lock the door, anyway?"

"I didn't lock the -"

Sighing again, he adjusted himself a little and leaned more squarely against the wall.

"Fine," he continued, "if you have to take the car, then just go. Don't worry about me, I can look after myself for an hour or so." He fidgeted again, only to stop as he felt the slicing pain in his side once more. "This is so stupid," he added. "I'm not hurt, not really. I should be able to get out to the car without any help."

"Yes, well, you can't," she said, turning and walking out of the room. "Don't worry, I shall be back before you even know that I'm gone. I'm sure it can't be *that* hard to drive a car."

He opened his mouth to tell her to stop fussing, before stopping as he realized what she'd just said. As he heard the front door opening and closing, he turned and looked out toward the hallway.

"You know how to drive, right?" he asked cautiously. "Mrs. Windermere? You've got an actual driving license, haven't you?"

He waited, and a moment later he heard the engine starting. Listening with a growing sense of concern, he heard the car slowly rumbling across the driveway, followed by the sound of something metallic clattering and banging, then by a heavy bump as if a car had gently hit the house itself. Then came a brief roar of the engine before the vehicle started moving away with a series of unsteady, intermittent bursts.

Finally, left in silence, Jonathan told himself that everything was going to be fine. There wouldn't be too many other drivers on the road at almost two in the morning and he was fairly sure that the route to the nearest village was more or less straight, so he figured that he had at most about one hour to kill before help arrived. He tried again to sit up, hoping that he might be able to at least explore the house a little more, but the pain was immediately too much.

"Damn it!" he hissed, before slamming a fist impotently against the wooden floor. "Why the hell did I ever stop here?"

CHAPTER FIFTEEN

A FEW MINUTES LATER, as a fox screamed again somewhere far off in the forest, Jonathan found himself staring at the hooks on the walls and replaying the incident with the dead animals.

He was fairly sure that any deer missing its skin must be dead, so he was struggling to work out exactly how the damn things had not only managed to appear without warning, but how they'd then fallen from the hooks and had made such a chaotic attempt to break out of the room. He looked over at the broken window and saw the sharp glass shards glinting in moonlight, but there was no sign of any blood.

And yet...

And yet he knew what he'd seen.

Those deer *had* been in the room, and the

pain in his ribs was more than enough testament to the fact that they'd been very real, yet somehow they'd left behind no obvious biological trace. Had they simply managed to flee before Patricia had forced the door open? And *how* had she managed to get into the room, anyway? The door had seemingly locked itself from both sides with no sign of a key, so why had neither of them been able to open it while the mysterious deer were causing so much havoc? And why was the light switch suddenly working? All these questions and more were percolating in his mind as he looked down at the floor and once again spotted his broken mobile phone.

All he could hope was that Rebecca was still asleep and that he'd be able to get home before she had a chance to wake up and worry that something might be wrong.

A moment later, hearing footsteps, he turned and looked into the hallway.

"Mrs. Windermere?" he called out. "Are you back? I didn't hear the car."

The footsteps continued, making their way closer, before stopping as abruptly as they'd started.

"Mrs. Windermere?"

Again, he heard no response.

"You didn't crash the car, did you?" he asked. "Do you actually know how to drive at all?"

He waited, convinced that she must have

returned, but over the next few seconds that sense of certainty began to ebb away. Although he could see no sign of anyone in the hallway, he knew that somebody had to be out there, and after a few more seconds he realized that perhaps he *could* see someone after all: he wasn't sure, but as he stared at the wall next to the foot of the staircase, he began to pick out what appeared to be the shadow of a person in the darkness.

"Hello?" he said cautiously, wondering whether somebody else might have strayed into the house instead. "Who's there?"

As the seconds passed, he began to feel more and more concerned – and more and more exposed. Looking around, he quickly realized that he had absolutely no way of defending himself, but he quickly focused on the fact that any new visitor was unlikely to be dangerous. Instead, he tried to concentrate on the possibility that this might actually be a good development and that he was no longer relying upon the somewhat erratic Patricia Windermere for help.

"My name is Jonathan Pearson," he said cautiously, "and... well, I'm not really supposed to be here, in case you're wondering. I met Mrs. Windermere – I don't know whether or not you know her – and she brought me here and, well, one thing led to another and now I've got fractured or maybe even broken ribs. She went to fetch help, but if you've got a phone, would you mind calling an ambulance?"

Waiting again, he kept his eyes fixed on the shadow – or at least, the possible shadow – on the wall at the other end of the hallway. The more he stared at the shape, the more he became convinced that it *was* the shadow of a person, although in the back of his mind he knew that such things could easily be mere tricks of the light. Gradually, as no answer came to his request for help, he began to accept that the shadow was merely a coincidence and that the supposed footsteps had been...

A hallucination?

A trick of the light?

Wishful thinking?

Reaching up, he touched his own forehead but felt no sign of a fever. He told himself that his best bet now was just to ignore the shadow, but at the same time he desperately wanted to prove the truth one way or the other. After a few seconds, he began to think that perhaps he could find a way to crawl to the doorway without causing too much pain in his ribs.

"Here we go, then," he whispered, before very slowly and very carefully rolling down onto his back.

He immediately felt the pain stirring in his chest, but this time he was able to stop it becoming anything too unbearable. Fully aware that he might be making the damage worse, he tilted his head back until he had an upside down view of the hallway, and he saw that the shadow was still in the same place. Taking a deep breath, he braced for the inevitable pain to come as he began to inch his way toward the door. For a moment he had to look down to make sure that his foot wasn't about to catch on the table, and then – when he looked out into the hallway again – he realized that the shadow was suddenly gone.

Stopping, he listened for any sign of movement, but he was already starting to feel foolish for letting his fears take control. He felt as if he was becoming precisely the kind of panic-filled paranoid idiot he'd always pitied.

The pain in his ribs was burning now and he knew he'd probably caused some more damage, but he figured that he'd be fine just as soon as he reached a hospital. At the same time, however, he was starting to taste blood in the back of his throat. Although he told himself that this sensation was caused by the fact that he'd rolled over, he couldn't help but also notice that he was feeling a little weaker than before.

"It's going to be fine," he said out loud, trying to make himself feel a little more confident. "You're not badly hurt, it's just... it's just pain."

Swallowing hard, he tasted more blood.

"Pain is the body's way of telling you that

there's a problem," he continued. "I know there's a problem, so the pain is... it's quite irrelevant. Got to be... logical about these things..."

As those words left his lips, his eyes began to slip shut. Immediately realizing that he needed to stay awake, he forced his eyes open again, only to quickly feel them wanting to close once more.

"You need to stay awake," he murmured. "Not a... not a good thing to go to sleep, not when you can taste blood. Probably fine, but... just in case..."

He blinked a couple of times, but slowly his eyes were closing once more and this time he told himself that there was no harm in just allowing himself to rest for a minute or two.

"Wake up!"

Startled, he opened his eyes and found himself still on his back in the doorway, partially in the hall of Lotham Lodge and partially in the old kitchen. He wasn't sure how long he'd been asleep, but he felt sure it could only have been a matter of seconds at most. His heart was racing now and he could still hear those two words ringing in his head, and after a moment he realized that he'd recognized the voice.

Rose.

No.

No, he knew it couldn't have been Rose. She was far away back at home and, as far as he knew, fast asleep in bed. Taking a deep breath and feeling a sharp pain in the process, he realized that he was perhaps a little more badly injured than he'd initially understood, and now all thought of sleep was well and truly out of his mind.

"You're going to stay awake," he said firmly, even though he knew he was already feeling even a little weaker than a few minutes earlier. "You just have to hold out until Patricia Windermere gets back with help."

Taking another deep breath, he realized that the pain was getting worse. Figuring that he could perhaps use that pain as a means of keeping himself awake, he told himself that he needed to roll over onto his side or perhaps even onto his front. He braced himself, ready for the agony, and then he rolled himself in one quick motion.

By the time he was on his side, he was already in absolute agony, but he used this sensation to force himself up until finally – contrary to his original plan – he was kneeling on the carpet in Lotham Lodge's hallway.

"So far, so good," he said under his breath, and he was relieved to find that the taste of blood was no longer quite as strong.

Feeling a little clammy, he wiped sweat from his brow as he tried to work out what to do next. He knew he was still too weak to go charging about, but he at least felt that he could have proved

Patricia wrong by making it to the car if only he'd make a little more effort. Not wanting to remain on his knees, however, he told himself that he could probably at least make it to a chair in the front room, so a moment later he reached out and grabbed the side of a dresser so that he could start pulling himself up.

And then he froze as he saw a short, balding man standing in the front room holding a glass of wine, staring back out at him with a puzzled expression.

CHAPTER SIXTEEN

"WHO -"

For a moment, Jonathan felt as if nothing made sense. As he stared at the man – and as the man stared back at him – he began to worry that his entire understanding of the world was slipping, as if he was hallucinating. He dimly remembered banging his head earlier, back when the deer had been attacking him, and now he worried that perhaps he was suffering from some kind of concussion. And as he tried again and again to figure out what was going on, he realized that both he and the strange man seemed locked in a silence that neither of them could break.

And then, finally, the man turned and walked away out of sight. As he did so, his footsteps clicked loudly through the open doorway.

Taking yet another deep breath, Jonathan tried to work out how to react next. The man had certainly noticed him but had clearly not been terribly troubled by his presence – beyond an obvious sense of bafflement, at least. That reaction in itself was clearly extremely strange, and already he was starting to wonder whether perhaps the vision of the fellow had been all in his mind. A few seconds later, however, he heard what seemed to be the clinking of glasses, and seconds after that a flickering warm glow began to light the room – as if a fire had been started in a hearth.

"Well?" a voice called out in a clipped, slightly old-fashioned and perhaps even posh English tone. "Are you going to stay out there all night?"

"Are... are you talking to me?" Jonathan asked cautiously.

"Who else might I be talking to?"

"I'm sorry," Jonathan continued, wincing in pain as he gripped the dresser's side and hauled himself up a little more fully. "Are you with Patricia?"

"Who?"

Realizing that standing in the hallway was getting him nowhere, Jonathan figured that he had to at least make it through to the front room. The pain in his ribs was still strong but he felt as if he was at least used to the discomfort by now, so as he began to carefully step forward he managed to avoid moving in a way that set off the worst of the agony. By the time he reached the open doorway he could feel a burning sensation in one side of his chest, and the niggling taste of blood wouldn't quite leave the back of his throat, but he figured that he was at least moving *slightly* better than before.

Any form of progress, he told himself, was better than remaining on the floor in a crumpled heap.

Looking into the room, he saw the man standing at the fireplace, staring into flames that appeared to have sprung up from nowhere.

"You seem to be in a bit of a state," the man murmured, not turning to look at him. "Been in the wars, have we?"

"The wars?"

"It's alright, you don't have to be brave," the man said, finally glancing at him with a smile. "We're all friends here, aren't we? Although you'll have to remind me of your name, I'm afraid. Are you one of Wally's friends? Or Bertie's? One of them brought you along for the weekend, didn't they?"

"What the hell are you talking about?"

"Oh, but I don't suppose it matters," the man chuckled, before heading over to a table in the corner and starting to pour a glass of wine, only to find that the bottle was empty. "Well, that's a blasted shame," he said, before craning his neck to look past Jonathan. "Mrs. Simmons? Mrs. Simmons! We're out of wine! I don't know how it's happened, but could you bring another bottle through? The same'll do! I need another bottle of this Chateau Something-or-Other."

He waited, and already he looked a little puzzled by something.

"I'm sure she heard me," he continued, furrowing his brow. "She's probably just busy. You know, I inherited her from my father and I'm sure she was a good servant for him but I find her terribly slow and frankly a little rude sometimes. Life can be terribly draining if one doesn't get along with one's housekeeper."

He marched to the doorway and looked through into the hall.

"Mrs. Simmons!" he yelled.

He waited, and Jonathan waited, but they both heard nothing but silence.

"Damn and blast it," the man continued. "Where is that woman? I know it's getting late but she should stay up until I retire. Or at least until I dismiss her for the night. Then again..."

He hesitated, before slowly turning to Jonathan as if he was a little confused.

"Then again," he added, "it *has* been quite the night, hasn't it?"

Jonathan tried to offer a faint smile, but the

effort immediately brought a burning shaft of pain into his ribs.

"I suppose the others have all gone home," the man said softly, with more than a hint of sadness in his voice, before turning and walking to the window. "Funny how that happens. You have one little mishap on a shooting expedition and – boom – they all suddenly remember that they have places to be. Don't think I didn't spot them scurrying away like rats leaving a ship. I called after them, I told them that there was no need to panic, but did that stop them? Of course it bloody didn't. Loyalty is a fine and important thing and when the chips are down one sees the truth about one's friends."

He looked out the window for a moment.

"I'm sorry," he said after a few seconds, "perhaps you told me but... what is your name again?"

"I was about to ask you the same thing," Jonathan said cautiously. "Are you here with Patricia Windermere?"

"I really haven't the foggiest idea who that is," the man said. "My name is Alfred. Lord Alfred Makepeace, although my friends call me Alfie. And you look like a nice fellow, I think we can be friends, you and I. Plus you're the only one who seems to have stuck around. And your name is..."

"Jonathan. Jonathan Pearson."

"Do you mind if I call you Johnny?"

"People don't usually."

"It sounds so much friendlier," Lord Makepeace replied with a forced smile. "You know, it's at times like these that a man starts to question his judgment. All those friends I invited here this weekend... I find myself wondering whether they were really my friends at all. Especially when they all ruddy fled the scene at the drop of a hat. But you've stayed, and we barely know each other. That makes me think that you must be a capital fellow."

"Makepeace," Jonathan whispered. "Lord..."

For a moment, he could only think back to Patricia's words from earlier.

"There's the old louche," she'd explained while looking at one of the paintings. "Lord Alfie Makepeace, late of this manor. The drunk who, if stories are to be believed, was responsible for Maurice's death. It certainly seems to be no coincidence that his family soon began to desert him."

"What is it?" Lord Makepeace said now, tilting his head slightly. "Why are you staring at me with such a queer look on your face?"

"So you're a descendant of the Makepeace family," Jonathan said cautiously.

"I am, as it happens, although sometimes I find the whole thing to be a dreadful burden. Do you happen to have ever had a great big country pile just dropped on your shoulders?"

"Can't say that it's ever happened to me."

"People think it's lucky, but if you ask me it's the most terrible burden," Lord Makepeace said, before heading to the table and starting to once again pour some wine, only to find that the bottle was still empty. "Darn it," he muttered, clearly confused, "Mrs. Simmons still hasn't been through, has she?"

"I don't think there's a Mrs. Simmons here," Jonathan replied, trying to ignore the increasingly painful burning sensation in his ribs. "Hey, you don't happen to have a mobile phone, do you?"

"A what?"

"I'm not sure I want to completely rely on Mrs. Windermere," he continued. "Is there any way you could call an ambulance for me?"

"Whatever for?" Lord Makepeace asked. "There's nothing wrong with you that a good stiff drink won't cure!"

He marched back across the room, once again stopping in the doorway.

"Mrs. Simmons?" he shouted, a little louder than before. "I say, Mrs. Simmons, a man could die of ruddy thirst in here waiting for you to show up! Is there any chance of that bottle of wine I asked for a while ago?"

Once again he waited, but the only response was the continued silence of the rest of the house. A moment later the wind blew the trees outside, causing a rustling sound, and Lord Makepeace spun around to look over at the window.

"Did you see anything?" he gasped.

"I'm sorry?" Jonathan replied.

"Out there," the older man continued, and now he seemed genuinely terrified. "I thought I heard something, that's all. I'm afraid I've entirely lost track of the time." He swallowed hard. "But it's so easy to get spooked, isn't it? I'm sure there's no reason to worry." He turned and looked out into the hallway again. "Mrs. Simmons! Where are you with that ruddy wine?"

CHAPTER SEVENTEEN

"THIS IS JONATHAN PEARSON, I'm afraid I can't come to the phone right now but if you leave a message I'll get back to you just as soon as I can."

"Where the hell are you?" Rebecca muttered, cutting the call and setting her phone down on the kitchen table. "It's almost two in the morning."

Sitting in silence for a moment, she tried to tell herself that there was no need to worry. She knew Jonathan was a good driver and in his messages he'd mentioned something about popping by to check on some house. As much as she wanted to tell herself that he was fine and that he could handle himself, however, part of her still worried that it was very unusual for him to run out of battery on his phone, and that he never turned the wretched thing off. Sure, he might simply be in a signal dead spot, but she didn't like relying on assumptions. And the more she sat and thought of reasons why he was almost certainly fine, the more she felt other thoughts creeping into her mind.

Tapping at her phone again, she brought up his first voicemail.

"Hey, so this is going to sound strange but I'm taking a brief detour on the way home to a place called Lotham Lodge. It sounds like it'd be right up your alley, actually. There's this woman who claims that it's haunted and... I mean, the whole thing has kind of dropped into my lap in some ways, so I figure I might as well give it a look. I'll probably be an hour or two later home. Don't wait up too long."

Sliding her laptop over, she opened the lid and brought up a browser window, and she quickly typed the name Lotham Lodge into a search engine. She came up with information about a house on some kind of larger estate, and she saw several photos of a small but rather grand-looking stone building that appeared to be set in a clearing in the middle of a forest. Scrolling down, she couldn't help but wonder why this place in particular would ever have attracted her husband's attention, but finally she found a section that made her stop.

"The ghosts of Lotham Lodge," she whispered, reading out loud from the page. "For years, rumors have persisted that the lodge is haunted by not one but two spectral presences. Outside in the garden and driveway, the terrifying vision of a dead gamekeeper has sometimes been spotted with his head badly damaged following a hunting accident. And within the house itself, some say that the ghost of Lord Alfred Makepeace – the very man who shot the gamekeeper – is sometimes to be heard stalking the corridors as he struggles with guilt."

Hearing a creaking sound, she looked over her shoulder and saw the bottom of the stairs.

"Alicia?" she said cautiously. "You're not up, are you?"

She waited but heard nothing, and after a moment she returned her attention to the laptop. The house was certainly old enough to occasionally creak and groan a little in the small hours.

"Those who dare to spend a night at Lotham Lodge often report hearing ghostly footsteps, especially downstairs in the old drawing room and the room at the front of the house where Lord Makepeace used to hold his infamous parties after the hunt. And some even claim to have spied the ghostly figure itself and to have heard him muttering away to himself. Is it a coincidence, then, that Lord Makepeace is said to have died in the lodge after seeing the ghost of his dead gamekeeper? Are these two men trapped together, haunting one another for eternity?"

Scrolling back up to the top of the page, she once again looked at a photo of Lotham Lodge.

"Two ghosts haunting each other," she said, raising both eyebrows. "I suppose that might grab Jonathan's attention, but..."

Looking at her phone again, she saw that the time was now 1:37am and that he still hadn't replied to any of her messages.

"What the hell are you up to out there?" she murmured under her breath. "You'd better have a damn good reason for going all quiet on me."

***

"She's settled again," Doctor Einshorn said, leaning over the bed and watching for a moment as Rose continued to sleep. "It's the strangest thing. There's no way she should have been able to wake up, not with the sedatives we've been giving her."

"Trust me, it happened," Henry said, watching from the foot of the bed. "She was going on and on about all this crazy stuff. None of it made any sense."

"We're going to have to run a battery of tests on her in the morning," Einshorn continued. "Or rather, someone else will, because I should have been out of here half an hour ago." Reaching down, he touched Rose's forehead with the back of his hand. "There's still no sign of a fever," he added, "so I'm not unduly concerned, but I don't like these seizures."

"What do you think's causing them?"

"If I knew that, I'd have started the treatment already."

"She kept saying that someone's in danger," Henry explained. "That someone needs help and we have to get him out of somewhere, but I really couldn't figure out who she was talking about. You don't think we should try to... figure that out, do you?"

"It was probably just nonsense," Einshorn suggested. "Besides, did she give you a name or any details?"

Henry shook his head.

"There's really nothing we can do except wait until morning and then get on with the tests." He took a look at his watch and hesitated for a moment, lost in thought, before letting out a faint sigh. "Damn it," he continued, "I'm half an hour over but I can't just walk away when this is happening. I guess I'll just have to stick around for another hour or so, just to make sure that she doesn't have another seizure."

"I could get one of the other -"

"I've made my decision," Einshorn added firmly, with the tone of a man who didn't expect to be challenged again. "It's just a precaution, and there's some paperwork I can be getting on with. I think -"

Suddenly hearing a bumping sound, he turned just in time to see a clipboard falling to the floor, having evidently dropped off the side of a nearby table. Stepping over, he picked it up and put it back in its place.

"I didn't like the way she was talking," Henry said, still watching Rose's sleeping face. "You should have heard her, she sounded so insistent. She kept going on and on about this need to save someone. I know you think it was just random rubbish, but I swear it sounded like she really meant it. Are you sure we shouldn't tell someone?"

"Tell them what?" Einshorn asked, heading to the door. "That a young girl on the ward made some vague comments while under the influence of sedatives and in the middle of a seizure? I'm sure the local police would rush to try to figure out what she was going on about."

"So we're going to do nothing?"

"No, we're going to keep her sedated until morning," Einshorn said, turning to him with an exasperated expression on his face. "That *is* doing something and -"

Before he could finish he heard a bump, and he turned to see that the same clipboard had once again slid off the same table. Hesitating, he looked around the room, trying to work out exactly what had happened, and then he made his way over and picked the clipboard up once more.

"It moved by itself," Henry said.

"What -"

"I saw it," Henry continued. "I swear, I know how crazy this sounds, but that thing moved by itself."

"How long have you been working tonight?"

"Almost twelve hours now, I'm covering but -"

"Then you're way past knocking off time," Einshorn said firmly. "Go on, get out of here. You're not fit to work if you're actively hallucinating."

"That clipboard -"

"I'm not listening," Einshorn replied, cutting him off and putting the clipboard back in place. "Seriously, I'm telling you to go home. I'll stick around for another hour just to make sure that the girl's okay, and then I'll write up a full report for the morning."

"What about her family?" Henry asked. "Should we inform them of the latest developments?"

"And worry them unnecessarily?" Einshorn thought for a moment. "No, the last thing we need is for them to rush back and start getting in the way with all their pesky emotional overreactions? They wouldn't be able to help and they might just cause more problems. There'll be time for all that in the morning. Once I'm out of here."

As Henry left the room, Einshorn continued to watch Rose. Stepping over to the bed, he looked down at her face and saw that her closed eyes were twitching, as if there was more activity that he would usually expect. He double-checked the sedative, and then – figuring that there was no need to obsess over minor details – he turned and made his way out of the room.

On the bed, Rose still had her eyes closed but after a few seconds her lips twitched, as if she was trying but failing to say something. Over on the table, meanwhile, the clipboard once again began to slowly slide toward the edge.

CHAPTER EIGHTEEN

"MRS. SIMMONS?" LORD MAKEPEACE shouted, stepping into the hallway and looking toward the top of the staircase. "Mrs. Simmons, this is quite intolerable! I called for wine several minutes ago and you haven't brought it! What's going on?"

"I really don't think there's a Mrs. Simmons here," Jonathan said, watching him from the doorway. "Then again, until a few minutes ago I didn't know *you* were here, either."

Looking back into the front room, he once again saw the portrait of the other, long dead Lord Makepeace. Making his way through, he approached the painting and stopped to take a closer look, and he had to admit that the resemblance to the man out there in the hallway was uncanny.

"I really ought to think about replacing her," Lord Makepeace said as he hurried through and went to check the wine bottle again. He seemed more agitated now, as if the lack of wine was making him nervous. Picking up the bottle, he checked once more that it was still empty, that it hadn't been miraculously refilled while he wasn't looking. "Perhaps she was good at her job once but she's bally well losing her touch now."

"So who exactly is this in the picture?" Jonathan asked. "How many greats removed are you from this guy?"

"Hmm?"

"I was just wondering about your position in the family."

"Oh, I don't have time for all of that now," Lord Makepeace murmured, hurrying instead to the window and once more looking out at the darkness. "You know, one of the most wonderful things about wine is the way that it calms the soul. When one is sober, on the other hand, one is perfectly aware of every last little thing going on in the world." He paused for a moment, as if he was contemplating the forest beyond the window. "One notices every rustle of the trees, every scratch against the window, every -"

Letting out a sudden gasp, he took a step back.

"Every... what?" Jonathan asked.

"Did you hear it?"

"I didn't hear anything."

"Then you must be deaf. Are all the doors sealed?"

"Alfred -"

"I must make sure!" Lord Makepeace stammered, hurrying out of the room. "Mrs. Simmonds, bring the wine and then help me seal the doors and windows! He can't be allowed to get inside!"

"This guy's nuts," Jonathan said under his breath. "These rich idiots usually are."

He listened to the sound of footsteps racing from room to room, and in truth he really wasn't sure what he was supposed to do next. He supposed that Patricia Windermere still wouldn't be back for a good while yet, so after a moment he lowered himself down and sat in one of the leather chairs. He quickly stood up again, however, as he realized that he might be in danger of falling asleep, which seemed to be a bad idea in the circumstances. And then, tasting blood again, he touched a finger against his lips, only to pull it away and spot a trace of blood.

"You're going to be fine," he said under his breath. "People don't die from cracked ribs. Just hold tight and you'll be at the hospital soon enough."

***

A couple of minutes later, as he realized that he'd heard no sign of Lord Makepeace for a good while now, Jonathan slowly inched his way out into the hall while wincing as he felt his damaged ribs cutting into his flesh.

He stopped and listened, but now the house seemed to be entirely still and silent.

"Hello?" he called out. "Lord Makepeace? I mean... Alfred?"

He waited.

"Alfie?"

Wondering where the crazy guy could have gone, he briefly considered going back into the front room. After a moment, however, he instead shuffled over to the foot of the stairs and looked up. He felt sure that he would have heard if the man had gone up there, yet he couldn't quite understand how or why such a panic-filled person could have suddenly stopped making any noise at all.

It was almost as if someone had used a switch to turn the man off entirely.

Slowly easing himself down onto the stairs, he told himself that he could afford to sit for a few minutes so long as there was no danger of falling asleep. The pain in his ribs was starting to throb now, and he could no longer deny that in general he was feeling much worse. Still, despite a complete lack of medical training, he felt sure that he wasn't too badly hurt and that – at most – he just needed to hang on until an ambulance showed up.

Already, however, he could feel himself starting to get tired again.

Suddenly footsteps hurried across the hallway, and he turned to see Lord Makepeace heading toward the front room. Something seemed slightly different about the man, however, even if he couldn't quite work out what.

"There you are," Jonathan said, before trying to get up.

Struggling a little, he had to make three attempts before he was on his feet, at which point he shuffled over to the doorway while trying to minimize the pain in his ribs.

"I wondered where you'd gone," he continued as he entered the room. "You went so -"

Stopping, he was shocked to see that while this was most certainly Lord Makepeace, the man now looked significantly older – as if a decade or so had passed in just the space of a few minutes.

"Did you hear anything out there?" the older man grumbled, once again peering out though the window.

"Are you okay?" Jonathan asked.

"What kind of bloody stupid question is that?" Lord Makepeace snapped angrily, turning to him with a much rounder and puffier face. "Damn it, where's that fool Charles with my wine? Sometimes he's so slow, he actually makes me regret firing that Simmonds woman."

"You got a new housekeeper?" Jonathan replied. "That was... quick."

"I don't know why I allow myself to get so worked up. It's just that I know what happens every year on this night, and always at precisely three minutes past one in the morning."

"You don't need to worry about that," Jonathan pointed out. "It's closer to two o'clock now."

"Hmm?"

Lord Makepeace stared at him for a moment, as if confused, before looking outside once more.

"No-one understands," he continued. "They don't know what it's like to have this... this burden on one's shoulders, and they certainly don't know what it's like to carry that burden for so bloody long. Year after year I have to deal with that ridiculous man showing up again, and for what? What does he even hope to get out of it? I always make sure that the doors and windows are all locked, just in case."

"You seem different," Jonathan pointed out.

"Different?"

"To earlier."

"My dear fellow, whatever are you

blathering on about?" Lord Makepeace replied. "I've never met you before. In fact, who are you? What are you even doing in my home?"

"You've never -"

Puzzled, Jonathan tried to understand exactly what could be making the strange man not only appear to age in a matter of minutes, but was also apparently messing with his memory.

"I don't get many visitors these days," Lord Makepeace continued, sounding a little sadder now. "Almost none, in fact. All my so-called true friends deserted me a long time ago after the unpleasantness. Even Mrs. Simmonds eventually announced that she'd obtained employment elsewhere. Of course, I immediately fired her, I wasn't even interested in having her work out her notice. When someone is gone, they should be gone immediately instead of lingering. Then I took Charles in, but in truth I struggled terribly to find someone who was willing to come and work for me at all. I might even admit that I was getting slightly desperate. People *do* love to gossip, don't they?"

He let out a heavy sigh.

"And Charles is a drunk," he added bitterly. "All I could find by way of a manservant was an alcoholic straight out of Pentonville. Can you believe that? I, a member of the House of Lords, reduced to hiring a common criminal to attend to my needs. Not that he bothers much, because he knows that I can't exactly replace him too easily. And all because of one foolish little mistake many years ago that, in truth, has never really mattered very much."

Jonathan waited, but now Lord Makepeace seemed to be lost in a world of his own. A moment later, before either of them could say anything, they both heard a loud thud against the house's front door.

"That's him!" Lord Makepeace gasped, turning and staring in horror at the hallway. "Don't let him in! Wait, he *can't* get in! But why does he come here, year after year? What draws him to the lodge? Can it really be a lust for vengeance?"

"Are you talking about that Maurice Wooden guy?" Jonathan asked, heading to the door and looking through into the hallway. "Patricia Windermere was going on about him too."

He turned to Lord Makepeace again.

"I really don't think that there's any -"

And then he froze as he saw, to his utter astonishment, that Lord Makepeace had once again seemingly vanished into thin air.

CHAPTER NINETEEN

"LORD MAKEPEACE?" JONATHAN CALLED out yet again, still looking around the room as he tried to ignore the growing pain in his ribs. "Where are you? Are you hiding?"

Stepping over to the chair in the corner, he half expected to find the wretched man cowering in fear, but already he was starting to realize that somehow he must have instead slipped out of the room. Ordinarily he might not have been too irritated by such behavior, but in that moment – as the pain in his ribs became stronger – he realized that he was rapidly running out of patience. Lord Makepeace seemed almost childish, and Jonathan Pearson had never enjoyed dealing with children too much.

Not even his own, sometimes.

"Where the hell is that woman with the ambulance?" he muttered, shuffling into the hallway and then stopping to look once more at the front door.

Telling himself that he needed to prove to himself that there was no ghostly figure, he headed to the door and pulled it open. Cold night air immediately blew against him, but – as he'd suspected – there was no undead former gamekeeper with a gaping wound in his head. Instead, all Jonathan saw was an empty porch and an equally empty driveway.

He waited for a moment, hoping against hope that he might spot vehicle headlights making their way closer, and then he shut the door and turned to set off in search of Lord Makepeace. He took a couple of steps forward, only for his knees to buckle at the last second. Dropping down, he let out a gasp of pain as he landed on all fours, and for a few seconds he felt strangely dizzy.

"Come on, pull yourself together," he whispered, trying to stay strong. "You're not -"

Suddenly he retched. Leaning forward, he was unable to stop himself bringing up the remains of his dinner from the conference, along with a splattering of bile. At the same time, the motion of vomiting brought a much sharper pain to his chest. He instinctively reached down and tried to touch his ribs, but the area felt swollen now and he winced as he had to pull his hand away.

"I'm fine," he stammered, wiping his lips as he forced himself to sit up. "It's all fine. There's no reason to worry."

Feeling clammy but also a little cold, he quickly realized that his damaged ribs must be more serious than he'd previously understood. He began to get to his feet, although he had to try a couple of times before finally managing to take several steps, at which point he stopped at an open doorway leading into some kind of storage room. Looking inside, he saw boxes filled with what appeared to be old items and trinkets from around the house, and his eyes quickly focused on something that he initially assumed must be some kind of mirage.

Stepping over to the box, he reached inside and pulled out an old-fashioned rotary telephone, complete with a receiver attached to a cradle and a curled mounting cord ending in a small plug. Somehow, miraculously, someone had evidently cleared the house out but had simply stored lots of items away. Having been so determined to find a mobile phone, he couldn't help but smile as he realized that it was a good old-fashioned landline phone that had come to his rescue.

"Finally some luck," he muttered, turning and taking the phone out into the hallway and then into the front room, hoping to spot a socket on one of the walls.

As he searched, however, he realized that his vision was becoming a little blurred, and he had to really focus in order to see properly. Even after he managed to clear his vision, he felt unsteady and he could sense that the nausea hadn't entirely gone away. Determined to call for help, however, he checked all around the room before heading back out into the hallway.

"If there's a phone," he said out loud, hoping to give himself a little more confidence, "then there has to be a jack somewhere."

He had to stop again to steady himself, and the nausea was now a constant presence in the pit of his belly, but for the first time since Patricia Windermere's departure he actually felt as if he was back in charge of his own situation. A moment later he spotted a phone jack on the wall, and as he made his way over he told himself that hopefully the line was still working.

And then, just as he was about to kneel down and test the phone, he heard a sudden loud knock on the front door.

Freezing for a moment, he looked at the door and told himself that perhaps the wind had caused the sound, or that maybe Patricia had finally returned with help. He listened, hearing only the sound of trees rustling outside, before finally he heard the knock again.

"Who's there?" he called out, thinking back

to all the warnings about Maurice Wooden.

He waited, but already he was starting to feel foolish. Finally he set the phone on the nearby table and made his way to the door, although he still hesitated after reaching out and touching the handle.

"Mrs. Windermere, is that you?" he asked.

Silence.

"Lord Makepeace, are you out there?"

No matter how hard he tried to tell himself that there was no reason to be fearful, somewhere at the back of his mind he couldn't help thinking about all the warnings. He knew that some long-dead gamekeeper wasn't about to appear at the house in the middle of the night, yet some part of him couldn't quite shake precisely that fear. He imagined a man standing on the other side of the door with not much of a head left, and then – in a fit of anger – he told himself to stop being so bloody stupid.

"This is ridiculous," he murmured, before pulling the door open. "You're letting these idiots get into your -"

As soon as he saw the porch, he let out a sigh of relief. There was absolutely no sign of anyone, and all he saw was the empty driveway. He immediately felt like a complete fool, although he reminded himself that he was quite badly hurt and that he was perhaps not entirely in full command of his faculties. And then, as if to add to the embarrassment, a large reddish-orange bird suddenly flew out of the darkness and landed hard against the wooden decking, causing exactly the same sound that he'd heard just a moment earlier.

"It was you, huh?" Jonathan said, watching as the bird hopped a little closer. Although he was no expert, the size of the creature – combined with the colorful red and green head – told him that it was probably a pheasant of some variety. "I don't mind admitting that you gave me a little fright, but let's keep that between ourselves, okay? There's no need to let anyone else know that I was such an idiot."

The bird looked up at him for a moment before turning, and in that moment Jonathan saw that one side of its body was bloodied and damaged, almost as if it had been shot.

"Are you okay there?" he asked, leaning down to get a better look.

The bird stayed perfectly still for a few seconds, and now Jonathan could see blood glistening in the matted feathers. He wasn't quite sure how any animal could still be alive after suffering such a major injury, but a moment later the bird turned to him and let out a brief, agonized cry.

"You're in pain, huh?" Jonathan said, feeling bad for the creature. "Well, maybe -"

Suddenly something slammed into the side of his head. Pulling back, he was shocked to see a second bird landing on the decking. This bird was an even larger pheasant, and it too was bloodied and wounded.

"Okay," he continued cautiously, "the wildlife round here really isn't too friendly. That's okay, though. You guys look like you've had it rough and -"

Before he could finish, another large bird landed, and this creature was missing almost one entire side of its body. A couple more pheasants landed nearby, and they too were suffering from a variety of injuries. Stepping back into the house, Jonathan watched as the birds stared back at him, and he couldn't help but feel a shiver pass through his bones as the first of them began to slowly made its way toward the door.

"I don't think you should be coming inside," he said cautiously, trying to keep from panicking while telling himself that his judgment was definitely impaired. "Just stay out there, okay?"

As if in response, the nearest pheasant let out a rattling cry, creating a sound that Jonathan felt sure shouldn't be coming from a healthy bird. Seconds later the other pheasants began to make their own cries, some of them bringing up blood that began to drip from their beaks.

"Stay back," he said firmly. "Don't -"

In that moment one of the birds shrieked and flew toward him, and Jonathan only just managed to slam the door shut in time. He felt a heavy weight slam against the door's other side, but he managed to put his weight against the wood and he listened as several pheasants cried out on the steps. A moment later, as he continued to push back against the door, he looked over at some shelves halfway up the stairs and saw half a dozen stuffed pheasants. For a few seconds he could only stare at them, until finally the roar of shrieks on the other side of the door came to an abrupt halt.

He waited, relieved by the silence, but a moment later he heard the distinct sound of a man clearing his throat somewhere else in the house. And then, after a few more seconds, he heard Lord Makepeace's voice once again.

"Help me," the man was gasping, sounding as if he could barely draw breath. "Please, someone... help me..."

CHAPTER TWENTY

"ALICIA."

Opening her eyes, Alicia found herself staring across her dark bedroom. She'd settled on the bed in an attempt to get to sleep, and finally – against the odds – she'd managed to drift off for a few minutes, only to wake up again as soon as she'd heard someone whispering her name.

Looking at her alarm clock, she saw the time.

1:56am.

For a few seconds she struggled to work out where the voice had come from, although after a moment she turned and looked over at the door, half expecting to see her mother. The light was still on at the bottom of the stairs, she could tell that much, but the house was silent and there was certainly no sign that anyone had entered the room. Sitting up, and pushing her favorite bear Mr. Anderson out of the way in the process, she suddenly remembered the small cut on her face. She touched her cheek, wondering whether the cut was real or whether it had been part of a dream, and she was just about able to feel a slight mark.

And that voice was still echoing in her mind, even as she began to recognize who it had belonged to.

"Rose?" she whispered, although she knew there was no way Rose could possibly have returned home already. "Are you here?"

She waited, but she heard nothing until – a few seconds later – her mother coughed somewhere downstairs.

More certain than ever now that she was alone, Alicia tried to focus on the idea that the voice had just been a dream, yet deep down she knew that it had been too clear and too distinct. A few seconds later she reached out and switched on her bedside light, but there was still no sign of anyone. And then, looking over at the window, she saw that the curtains were drawn but that there appeared to be just the faintest hint of a shape hiding behind one side.

"Rose?" she said again, before slowly crawling across the bed so that she could get a better view.

As soon as she reached the other end of the bed, she saw a pair of bare feet poking out from beneath one of the curtains. She immediately froze, feeling absolutely certain that nobody should be there, but already she could see that the feet were fairly small and that they most likely belonged to someone very young.

"Rose, is that you?" she continued, trying to reassure herself that nothing too strange was happening. "Rose, how did you come home? Does Mummy know?"

As soon as those words left her lips, she knew that the question was foolish. There was simply no way that Rose could have made it all the way back from the hospital alone, and there was also no way she could have got into the house without someone unlocking the front door. Still, the fact that she now appeared to be hiding behind the bedroom curtains seemed more than a little odd, and Alicia couldn't shake the feeling that she should probably go and fetch her mother.

Before she could do so, however, she realized that she could hear a faint sound, almost as if...

"Are you whispering?" she asked.

The sound continued, and after a moment Alicia climbed off the bed. She couldn't quite make out what Rose was saying, but she figured that it must be something important so she began to step across the room. By the time she reached the curtains, she was just about able to make out some of the words.

"He has to break the blood," Rose was saying softly. "It's been there now for far too long."

"What are you talking about?" Alicia asked, reaching out to pull the curtain aside. "What -"

"No," Rose said suddenly, "don't look at me."

"But -"

"Don't look at me!" Rose said again, much more firmly this time. "I don't know why, but I can't... I can't change it, so just don't look. Please."

Alicia hesitated, with her hand already touching the edge of the curtain, but finally she pulled back a little.

"Tell him to break it," Rose continued, sounding a little more urgent than before. "It's the only way. It's the blood that keeps pulling the man back to the house. It's the blood that was put there years ago like..."

She fell silent for a moment.

"Like a curse," she added finally, "but I don't know if it was meant to be a curse."

"Why are you talking about curses?" Alicia asked. "Rose, are you feeling okay? Why are you standing behind the curtain? Why are you even in my room?"

"I can't stay long," Rose said, and now her

voice was a little quieter than before. "They'll notice if I'm gone for too long, the machines will start making lots of noise. Please, it's so hard for me to be here at all, but you have to warn him. He has to break the blood into little pieces."

"What blood?" Alicia replied. "You can't break blood. Rose, you're not making sense."

Again she reached out to pull the curtain aside.

"Don't!" Rose hissed. "You can't look at me right now!"

"Why not?"

"Have you told him yet?"

"I don't know what you -"

"Why haven't you told him?" Rose snarled, sounding angrier and louder now. "He doesn't have much time left! That thing is going to the house again and it'll hurt him! It always hurts people when it finds them! The times aren't lining up but it's going to happen anyway!"

"Rose, what are you talking about?" Alicia sighed, before pulling the curtain aside. "Why -"

***

Still sitting on the sofa downstairs, with her laptop on her knees, Rebecca continued to search online for any news about traffic accidents or anything else that might explain why Jonathan was so late getting home. Her phone was on the arm of the sofa, but she'd tried her husband several more times and still hadn't been able to get through. As much as she wanted to stay calm, the time was now almost two in the morning and she couldn't understand why he hadn't at least been in touch to let her know what was happening.

"Come on, Jonathan," she whispered, "this isn't like -"

Suddenly she heard a scream. Pushing the laptop aside and letting it fall to the floor, she hurried out into the hallway and raced up the stairs.

"Alicia?" she shouted, stumbling slightly but managing to keep going as she rushed into her daughter's bedroom. "Are you okay?"

"Mummy!"

Slamming into her mother, Alicia put her arms around her tight and sobbed loudly. As she looked around the room, however, Rebecca saw nothing but the crumpled sheets on the bed with Mr. Anderson resting on a pillow, and then a moment later she noticed that one of the curtains had been pulled all the way aside.

"Make her stop!" Alicia cried, hugging her mother tighter and tighter. "Please!"

"What are you talking about?" Rebecca asked. "Alicia, I think you must have had a nightmare."

"It wasn't a nightmare!"

"Sweetheart, it's been a crazy night for both of us. Listen, why don't we go over to the bed and sit down? And then I'm pretty sure you'll realize that you just had a really nasty dream."

She tried to walk across the room, but Alicia was still holding her far too tightly. Finally she managed to move her daughter gently to the side, and in that moment she saw tears streaming down the girl's blustery red face.

"Sometimes nightmares feel very real," she told her, moving some strands of hair away from her daughter's eyes. "But that's all they are, they're nightmares and they can't hurt us."

"It was Rose!"

"Rose? What do you mean?"

"Rose is here!" Alicia shouted, turning and pointing toward the window. "I saw her!"

"Sweetheart, Rose is still at the hospital," Rebecca explained. "You remember that, don't you? She might be able to come home tomorrow but -"

"She was right there!" Alicia cried, barely able to get any words out at all as she continued to sob. "She was hiding behind the curtain and she was talking about breaking blood, and she wasn't making any sense and she told me not to open the curtain but I did and..."

She froze for a moment, as if she couldn't quite believe whatever had happened next.

"And her face was all wrong," she added

finally, looking up at her mother with pure fear in her eyes. "Mummy, part of her face was gone and there was lots of blood everywhere, and I could see bits of her skull. She only had one eye left and it was staring at me, but it was almost white and there was more blood coming out of her mouth. And she told me to warn Daddy, she said his name right before you came in and she said that he has to break some blood. But I don't know what she was talking about." She paused for a moment, sniffing back more tears. "Mummy, is something wrong with Daddy?"

CHAPTER TWENTY-ONE

"HMM, WHAT?"

Opening his eyes, Jonathan realized that he'd momentarily allowed himself to lose consciousness. He was sitting on a chair in the hallway of Lotham Lodge, and after a few seconds he remembered that he'd suddenly felt extremely weak; lowering himself onto the chair, he'd promised himself that he was only going to rest very briefly in order to get his strength back, but instead he'd allowed his eyes to close.

And then...

And then something had caused him to stir.

"Is this how it's going to be?" he heard a voice gasping, and now he remembered that he'd heard Lord Makepeace calling for help. "Is he finally going to get me?"

AMY CROSS

Hauling himself up, Jonathan somehow managed to shuffle across the hallway. He had to reach out and steady himself with each step, and the burning pain in his ribs was stronger than ever, but finally he was able to shuffle all the way to the door leading into the kitchen, and he saw Lord Makepeace sitting slumped at the table with his head in his hands.

Moonlight was shining through the window, picking out the panels in the stained glass portrait of one of the lord's ancestors. At least, Jonathan assumed that it must be one of his ancestors, even if the resemblance was more than a little uncanny.

"I should have known that eventually he'd get me," Lord Makepeace muttered darkly, before lowering his hands and looking at Jonathan, revealing a bloated face that was somehow even older than earlier. "Why did I even bother to fight it?"

"What... what happened to you?" Jonathan asked, stepping into the room and marveling at the fact that in the space of less than an hour the man had seemingly aged by a couple of decades. "Is this some kind of allergic reaction?"

"Every damn year I knew he'd come," the old man sneered, "yet every damn year I forced myself to sit here and try to prove him wrong. Why? Why did I waste all that time? I always swore that I didn't feel any guilt about what happened to the fellow, but now I wonder..."

His voice trailed off for a moment, and then slowly he turned and looked up at the window.

"How easily a life can crumble," he murmured. "It was all taken out of my hands, rather. Looking back I see how I could have stopped it all, but at the time... at the time I thought I was making all the right choices. Yet now look at me, sitting here all alone, abandoned even by that wretched criminal Charles. He took everything he could fit into his pockets. I tried to find myself another manservant, you know, but finances are a little strained and besides... it's as if nobody these days wants to work for me at all. I have been left to fend for myself. The bastard is due back any day to collect the last of his belongings, and probably half of mine as well."

"Does your phone line still work?" Jonathan asked.

"I'm sorry?"

"Your phone," he said again, allowing the pain to make him sound just a little more irritated than before. "It still works, doesn't it?"

"I think I hear him," Lord Makepeace replied, turning and looking at the window. "He treads softly but he comes ever closer. There's something so bloody righteous about the fellow. He was like that when he was alive, but in death he's so much worse and -"

Stopping suddenly, he winced as if he was in pain. Reaching up, he touched his left arm and began to rub it just below the shoulder.

"Are you feeling okay?" Jonathan asked cautiously.

"It wears one down terribly," the older man murmured. "One doesn't even notice, necessarily, until it all arrives in one's lap at once. I have felt for some months that tonight was to be the final night, and now I believe I am correct. Still, there is at least some blessed relief in the knowledge that I am to be spared another occurrence of this awful ritual. I can only hope that I myself am not forced to remain in this world as a ghostly presence. I would so hate to haunt the living."

He began to slowly rise from his seat, although he seemed more than a little unsteady and he almost tripped on the chair's legs as he stepped around to the far end of the table. Still rubbing his arm, he leaned against another chair as sweat ran down his face.

"But I shan't give him the satisfaction!" he snarled. "No, I shan't let him see me like this! I don't know what has drawn him here year after year, but if it is merely the hope that he can torment me, then after tonight he might as well leave forever! If he means to drag me down to the fiery pits of Hell, then I shall gladly go... for anything will be better than my life here."

"I'm sure it's not that bad," Jonathan replied, already feeling himself tiring again. "Listen, if -"

Letting out a sudden gasp, Lord Makepeace dropped down onto his knees.

"Are you sure you're okay?" Jonathan asked, shuffling toward him. "You're not -"

Before he could finish, the old man slumped down out of sight. Hurrying as fast as he could around the table, Jonathan was about to ask him again whether he was alright, only to stop as he saw that once again the man had vanished. This time he was absolutely certain that he couldn't possibly have found any way to sneak out of the room, yet there was no doubting the fact that one moment he'd been there and the next...

"He was found dead in the kitchen," he remembered Patricia explaining. "Right under the stained glass portrait of himself, I believe. His former servant returned for his belongings and found him one morning. There were stories that he'd died of fright after witnessing Maurice's ghost returning one night, but of course one never truly knows what went on, does one? I checked it out, though, and the death certificate certainly makes fright sound like a possible cause."

Staring at the spot where he felt sure Lord Makepeace must have fallen, Jonathan began to consider the possibility that he'd seen the man's ghost – or, rather, three separate ghosts of the same man seemingly torn from three very different stages of his life. And as much as he wanted to dismiss that idea out of hand, he couldn't ignore the fact that the man had somehow managed to keep disappearing from sight in ways that seemed utterly impossible. He wanted to come up with some kind of rational explanation, but a moment later he looked at the empty hooks on the opposite wall.

Thinking back to the sight of the dead deer – and they *had* been dead, he had no doubt of that fact now – he realized that he was all out of rational explanations.

He turned and looked at the window, where a large section remained broken with shards catching the moonlight. The section containing Lord Makepeace's image in stained glass, however, was very much intact, and for a few seconds Jonathan couldn't help but stare at the rather masterful recreation of the man's features. Making his way over, he looked up at the glass more closely. Although he didn't know a lot about stained glass, he could tell that this particular piece had been created by a master and he couldn't help but wonder how the likeness could possibly be so accurate.

Reaching up, he touched some of the panels and felt their slightly mottled surface as he felt a sense of awe and -

Suddenly he heard a loud knocking sound on the front door. Turning, his first thought was that the pheasants had returned, but somehow this sound had seemed more distinctly human. He waited, and after just a couple more seconds he heard the knock again, and now he was absolutely certain that someone was out there.

Checking his watch, he saw the time:

2:03am.

"You're an hour late," he whispered. "A little tardy for a ghost."

A moment later he heard the knock once more.

"Wait!" he shouted, although he was too weak to raise his voice above much more than a croaked whisper. "I'm coming!"

Hobbling around the table, barely able to put one foot in front of the other, he told himself that this was no ghostly visitation, that instead rescue had finally arrived. Just as he reached the doorway, however, his knees buckled and he fell, landing hard on the floor. For a few seconds he was barely able to see properly, and a moment later a small trickle of blood ran from his lips. As much as he'd been telling himself that his damaged ribs weren't too much of a problem, he knew now that he needed urgent medical help so he tried to stand, only to find that the effort required was too great.

"Hold on," he groaned, ruing the fact that he'd bolted the door while trying to keep the ghostly pheasants out. "Wait a moment."

Unable to stand, he instead began to crawl across the hallway, determined to reach the door.

"Patricia, is that you?" he tried to call out. "Did you fetch help? I've got to admit, I'm... I'm not in a very good way right now. I think you were right to go and find someone."

Although his progress was slow and painful, he forced himself to keep going until he reached the empty chair next to the door. Dragging himself up, he reached out with a trembling hand and just about managed to get the bolt out of the way, and then he grabbed the handle and began to pull the door open. As he did so, he happened to notice that the time on his watch was still three minutes past two o'clock in the morning.

"I need help," he stammered. "I don't think I'm -"

In that moment he froze as he saw a figure standing on the other side of the door. Wearing what appeared to be some kind of old-fashioned tweed, the man was covered in splattered blood while one entire chunk of the top of his head appeared to have been entirely blown away.

CHAPTER TWENTY-TWO

One hundred and eleven years earlier...

"WHY ARE YOU LETTING that dreadful man drag you out again?" Anne Wooden asked, unable to hide a sense of irritation as she sat on a stool in her workshop and continued to clean another pane of stained glass. "He never lets you have a day off, Maurice!"

"The master's had some friends come down to the house," her husband replied. "They can't very well go out hunting without me, can they? Can you imagine how that'd go? They'd never find a damn thing to shoot."

Reaching down, he let the dog eat from his hand.

"I don't see why they have to go hunting at

all," Anne said, rolling her eyes. "Can't they find any other ways to amuse themselves? Why must they always be out there killing innocent creatures?"

"Why the fuss?" he asked with a faint smile. "It's not as if you're free today. When's the last time you took so much as a morning off?"

"I'm running behind," she admitted as she held the piece of blue glass up and examined it in the morning light. "This is no good, I'm going to have to make some more from scratch."

"You're such a perfectionist."

"I have no choice," she said, getting to her feet and heading over to the furnace. "I shall have to light this again. It's going to add so much more time to the whole project, but I suppose time's one thing we have plenty of. Besides, I know Lord Makepeace wasn't keen on hiring me for this work. He only agreed to give me a chance because you and I came as a package." She sighed. "Then again, I shouldn't be too ungrateful. He *did* stump up the money to let me get this thing and create my own pieces from scratch."

"You'll be fine here without me today," Maurice said, stepping over to her and kissing the side of her face. "Give it five minutes and you won't even notice that I'm gone."

"Just promise me one thing," she replied, turning to him. "Promise me that when I've finally finished all this restoration work for that horrible man, you'll tender your resignation and we can go somewhere else. Just the two of us, together as man and wife."

"Where?"

"Anywhere, Maurice," she continued, and now she seemed almost to be begging him. "I don't mean to be immodest, but I'm sure I can obtain more commissions, and you'll be in high demand as a groundskeeper and game warden. We don't have to sit around here at this wretched lodge for the rest of our lives, do we?"

"Of course not," he said, before kissing her on the forehead. "If you think about it, *you're* the one keeping us here. How long did you say it was going to take you to make these windows for him? A year? Now it's been three and you're still talking about creating more glass. You might not want to admit it, Anne, but your determination to make everything perfect is what's really stopping us leaving."

"I just want to show everyone that I'm the real deal," she told him. "That my work is as good as anything produced by any man. I want to be seen as a real artist."

"And you shall be," he said as he heard voices out in the driveway. "But now, if you'll excuse me, there are pheasants that need shooting. From what I've seen so far, this latest batch of hunters seem to be the most impatient yet. These city people don't have the first clue about life out here."

***

"There's nothing so satisfying," Lord Makepeace opined several hours later, as he and the rest of the hunting party made their way through the forest, "as eating an animal that one has killed oneself. It's a feeling that harkens back to the most basic of instincts in all of us, to some deep connection to our old cave-dwelling lifestyles. It's good to know that such elements are still within us all. Why, just last week I had Mr. Wooden's wife Anne cook the leg of a deer I shot barely twenty feet from here."

"Are you sure there are pheasants out here?" one of the other men asked skeptically. "Call me crazy, but this doesn't seem like a very promising spot."

"Oh, it's full of life," Lord Makepeace said as he fiddled for a moment with his shotgun. "They try to hide but my gamekeeper knows how to flush them out."

"Careful with that thing," another man interjected.

"I know how to handle a weapon," Lord Makepeace said with a faint chuckle. "Wooden, tell these fellows how good I am at hunting and shooting. And fishing too, as it happens."

"His Lordship is a fine hunter," Maurice said, glancing at the men before looking ahead again as he tried to work out where best to stop.

The dog ran on ahead, quickly disappearing into the bushes.

A moment later, hearing a rustling sound, Maurice turned to see that a pheasant was caught in one of the snares he'd put out for wild rabbits. He immediately stepped over, meaning to free the poor creature, only to hesitate as he saw that he was too late: although the pheasant was still frantically trying to pull itself free, the bird had in the process almost ripped one of its wings off, while part of the wire had severely scratched and damaged its feet. As the pheasant let out a pained cry, Maurice made his way round to the other side and crouched down, before grabbing the dying animal by its neck and wringing it hard, hastening the moment of death and ending any suffering.

"My word," one of the men said, having watched the whole scene as it played out, "that was rather brutal. Couldn't anything have been done to save it?"

"Is it still cookable?" another man added.

"They don't usually go anywhere near the snares," Maurice muttered as he carefully pulled the carcass free. "I don't know why this one did."

"Maurice has a rare and rather special touch

with the creatures of the forest," Lord Makepeace observed. "A kind of sympathy, I suppose you might say. And they love him in return. From the smallest mouse to the largest deer, the animals all around here seem to respect Maurice a great deal."

"How weird," the first man muttered.

Having removed the dead pheasant, Maurice set it down gently on the ground.

"He's not going to give it a full burial, is he?" one of the men whispered.

"Maurice respects the natural world and its rules," Lord Makepeace replied. "He'll leave it out and something or other'll turn it into lunch. He's got some silly rule that we don't eat things we simply find. Only things we kill."

Getting to his feet, Maurice stepped past the snare and rejoined the others before marching ahead into the forest.

"Should we follow him?" a man asked.

"He's the only one who knows where we're bloody going," Lord Makepeace admitted, setting off after Maurice as the other men joined him. "Once we're away from the house, I always bow down to Maurice Wooden's superior knowledge. Sometimes I think that the forest is almost part of him. Part of his soul, if you will."

"You're always trying to be a poet, Alfie, aren't you?"

"I merely try to see the beauty in the world

around me," Lord Makepeace protested. "There's nothing wrong with that, is there? You know, since I left London far behind I've found myself becoming far more philosophical. You fellows should try that some time, it really is the most remarkable change of pace and -"

Suddenly he turned and look to his left. Raising his gun, he watched the bushes, and a few seconds later the other men began to slowly raise their weapons as well.

"What is it, Alfred?" one of them asked. "Did you hear something?"

"Maybe," Lord Makepeace said, before slowly lowering his gun. "No, perhaps not. I don't know, sometimes I just get rather startled out here. One never knows what one might come across, does one?"

"You're a strange one, Alfred Makepeace," another man murmured. "I was told you could be a bit of an oddball and that has certainly turned out to be the case."

"I'm not an oddball," Lord Makepeace replied, clearly slightly irritated by that suggestion. "It's quite something, isn't it? I invite you fellows to come out and enjoy my hospitality for the weekend, and you repay me by calling me all sorts of names. I don't expect undying fawning gratitude, exactly, but it *would* be nice to be taken seriously, at least."

"Oh, we all take you seriously, Alfred,"

another of the men chuckled. "There's no need to get your undergarments all in a twist about that."

"I'm not getting my -"

"This way!" Maurice called out suddenly from up ahead, waving at them. "Don't lag too far behind or I'm liable to lose you. We'll be shooting before too long."

"Let's just try to enjoy ourselves," Lord Makepeace said firmly as he tried to ignore the sense that he was being gently mocked. "And how many times do I have to tell you all? There's no need to call me Alfred, it's so terribly formal. Please, all my friends call me Alfie."

CHAPTER TWENTY-THREE

"THERE!"

Turning slightly to his left, one of the men raised his gun and fired just as several birds flew up from the nearby bushes. One of the birds immediately fell back down, and the man let out a satisfied cry as he lowered his gun again.

"I'm rather good at this!" he exclaimed as he watched the dog grabbing the dead pheasant and carrying it over to Maurice. "That looks like a very plump bird," he added. "I imagine it'll cook up jolly well."

"Everyone here seems to be a good shot," another man pointed out. "Well, except for our host."

"Don't you worry about me," Lord Makepeace murmured as he continued to examine his gun. "I've got more experience in these things than I've had hot dinners. I'm just a little concerned that this gun isn't quite firing straight. Maurice, you haven't given me a dud, have you?"

"Let's see," Maurice replied tersely, showing no sign that he was particularly impressed by his employer's excuses. Making his way over, he took the gun rather roughly from the man's hands and checked it over for a moment before handing it back. "Looks fine to me."

"Poor Alfred," a man nearby chuckled. "Always making excuses. He'd be a champion in any competition where excuses scored points!"

"It's not an excuse!" Lord Makepeace snapped. "I'm just attempting to ascertain that my tool for the job is up to scratch. At least I know a thing or two about guns. Not like the rest of you."

"All this shouting's no good," Maurice said dryly. "You'll be scaring away every pheasant for half a mile around."

"That's a good point," another man replied. "Shouldn't we all be a little quieter?"

"Now you're *all* ruddy experts, eh?" Lord Makepeace said. "Sometimes I really wonder why I bother being such an excellent host. Most of the time I merely get everything thrown straight back in my face."

"Calm down, old chap," the man next to him said, before slapping him hard on the shoulder.

"We're just joshing with you, that's all. You need to learn to not take yourself quite so seriously."

"Shall we proceed?" Lord Makepeace asked, turning to Maurice. "I feel a chill in the air and I really don't think we want to be out all day, do we? Besides, we need to get back in time to let your wife cook one of these fine birds." He turned to the others. "Maurice's wife Anne is a woman of many talents, and one of those talents is the ability to roast a pheasant to absolute perfection."

"This way," Maurice said, stepping past him and heading deeper into the forest, with the dog running alongside him. "Mind that you try to keep your voices down, though. Too much chattering'll drive the birds away."

"Do you really let him talk to you that way?" one of the men asked as he walked past Lord Makepeace. "I wouldn't let any servant of mine be quite so direct. You really ought to remind him who's in charge."

***

"Over there!"

Turning, Lord Makepeace took a moment to aim before pulling the trigger twice. Two more pheasants had been beaten out of the bushes, but both birds were able to make good their escape as chunks were blown from the sides of a pair of entirely innocent trees.

"*Another* miss, Makepeace?" a man said, no longer bothering to hide his mirth. "I was worried I'd be the worst shot out here today, seeing as how I've never handled a gun before, but clearly I shouldn't have been concerned."

"It's this bloody gun!" Lord Makepeace snarled, turning the weapon around again and making a great show of examining the trigger. "Something's off in the mechanism."

"You could get your man to check it," another man suggested. "Again."

At this comment, the rest of the hunting party began to laugh.

"Evidently there has to be something amiss," Lord Makepeace said, sweating a little now as he continued to try to find something wrong with the trigger. "I don't expect the rest of you to understand, but for a decent hunter even the slightest misalignment can cause serious problems. Why, if the trigger pulls even a millimeter or two to one side or the other, that would completely put me off."

Two of the men rolled their eyes.

"Maurice, would you check that gun for him again?" one of them asked. "He seems utterly convinced that it's to blame for his pathetic marksmanship."

Having made his way past the next bushes,

Maurice turned and looked back. His dog had caught up to him, wagging its tail eagerly as it waited for its next instruction.

"There's nothing pathetic about my marksmanship," Lord Makepeace sneered. "Listen, a joke's a joke but I really think you all ought to stop sniping at me. This is my forest and you're all using my guns, and it's my gamekeeper who's leading us out here and my animals that we're all shooting."

"*Trying* to shoot," a man murmured.

"Who said that?" Lord Makepeace shouted, turning to them as his face become red and very blustery. "What makes you think you can insult a man on his own land?"

"Alright, calm down a little," another man said, unable to stifle a smile as he slowly shook his head. "We're only having fun, Alfred."

"It's Alfie!" he screamed. "Why can't any of you get that into your thick heads? My friends call me Alfie!"

"Yes, but we're not really your friends, are we?" one of them pointed out. "I mean, I suppose that sounds rather harsh now that I think about it, but *friend* is rather a strong word."

"So this is how I'm to be repaid," Lord Makepeace continued, becoming redder in the face than ever. "What a fine spectacle of humanity I seem to have invited to join me here this weekend.

What contemptible specimens are gathered here before me."

"Steady on."

"I have every right to be taken seriously!" Lord Makepeace shouted. "Especially on my own land! Any real gentleman should know that, but perhaps I have invited entirely the wrong class of fellow this weekend! You're not even very good with your guns, are you? To be perfectly honest with you all, I've been deliberately missing quite a lot of my shots because I didn't want to make you feel bad for being so lousy, but now I'm starting to wonder why I ever -"

Suddenly hearing a rustling sound, he turned and raised his gun. In that instant, determined to prove to everyone that he was a far better shot than they realized, he pulled the trigger and fired. As he did so, at the very last second, he saw Maurice stepping into view.

In an instant, Maurice turned to one side as part of his face exploded, splattering blood against the bark of a nearby tree.

As the echo of the gunshot hung in the air, everyone fell silent and Lord Makepeace slowly lowered his weapon.

Maurice was somehow still standing, although a moment later he turned again to reveal that one eye was missing along with part of his skull.

Blood was running freely from the gaping wound, soaking the side of his neck; he took a step forward, then a second – far shakier – step, and then he stopped again before slowly dropping down onto his knees.

"You shot him," one of the men whispered.

"I thought he was a deer," Lord Makepeace stammered, taking a step back, "or... or a pheasant."

"You shot him," another man repeated.

Still on his knees, leaning against his own gun to hold himself up, Maurice opened his mouth as if he was trying to say something. More blood ran from his lips, but the only sound that emerged was a faint gurgling clicking sound.

"Should we... call for someone?" a man asked.

Unable to stop staring at his gamekeeper, Lord Makepeace let his own mouth hang open. The forest had fallen entirely silent now, yet somehow Maurice remained on his knees even as his blood began to dribble down against the leaves and mud; he swayed slightly, yet he seemed determined to remain upright for as long as possible. The dog, meanwhile, had finally returned and was already pawing at him and whining as if desperately trying to make everything better.

"I thought you were a deer," Lord Makepeace said finally, keeping his gaze fixed on Maurice's one remaining eye. "I swear, I... I thought you were..."

His voice trailed off, and a moment later Maurice finally succumbed. Falling to one side, he landed hard against the forest floor as the dog whimpered and pawed more frantically at his shoulder.

"I thought he was a deer," Lord Makepeace continued, staring straight ahead as the other men remained silent. "I thought... I mean, it's not my fault. It was a simple accident. You all made me so angry, I just... I thought he was a deer."

CHAPTER TWENTY-FOUR

"WE'RE OFF, ALFRED."

Sitting slumped in a chair in his drawing room, Lord Makepeace stared straight ahead as a fire crackled in the hearth.

"Did you hear me?" the man in the doorway continued. "We're all calling it a day rather early, I'm afraid. Best to hit the road and try to reach London as soon as possible. I mean, after what happened, we thought..."

He hesitated, aware that he didn't seem to be getting through to his host.

"Listen," he added finally, stepping into the room, "we all know it was an accident. These things happen and there's no need to ruin a chap's life just because of one little misdemeanor. We all trust that you'll sort it out and that you'll make the fellow's widow right. To be honest, we don't really want to be associated with any of this unpleasantness, so you don't need to worry about us gossiping once we get back to London. I think we all really just want to forget that this weekend ever happened."

Again he waited, but in Lord Makepeace's eyes he saw only a glazed expression.

"But you'll do the right thing, won't you?" he asked. "Alfred? I hate to think of the poor fellow's corpse still out there in the forest. I know the dog seemed determined to stay with him, but it's not right that he should be left on the ground like that. And you'll have to go out to that little house and tell his wife. So long as you do the right thing by them, I think the rest of us can rather leave it as settled business. We can't say fairer than that, can we?"

Flinching slightly as he remained in his chair, Lord Makepeace was unable to stop reliving the shooting over and over in his mind.

"Jolly good, then," the man said, turning and leaving the room. "We'll let you get on with the tidying up. And don't beat yourself down about this too much, Alfred. Everyone makes mistakes. We all know it wasn't deliberate. People like us don't go around shooting good gamekeepers willy nilly, do we? Where would be the sense in that?"

"It's Alfie," Lord Makepeace said after a moment. "My friends call me Alfie."

"Lord Makepeace?"

Footsteps hurried to the door, and a moment later Anne stopped to look in at him.

"I'm sorry to disturb you," she said, struggling as usual to remember the proper etiquette, "but I just saw that you'd all returned and that your guests appear to be leaving. Is that correct, Sir? Will there be no need for a large feast tonight? Did you bring back anything that needs preparing?"

She waited for a reply, but already she was starting to sense that something must be wrong.

"Lord Makepeace?" she continued cautiously. "Sir, I'm sorry, I must ask... where is Maurice?"

***

"It's so dark out there," she said several hours later, long after she'd served dinner for her employer. Now she was standing at the window of the dining room, looking out at the moonlit forest. "Sir, Maurice never stays out this long. I'm worried that something must be wrong."

She looked at the clock on the far wall.

"It's one in the morning," she added fearfully. "Why would he stay out so late? Something *has* to be wrong!"

"Wrong?" Lord Makepeace replied, having barely touched the food on his plate. He made a brief attempt to fake a yawn, although the effect was rather unconvincing. "What could possibly be wrong?"

"I don't know," she said, turning to him, "but Monty hasn't returned either. That dog sticks to Maurice's side with such loyalty." She stepped over to the table again. "What did you say Maurice was doing, again? You mentioned something about him checking some traps or -"

"Traps," Lord Makepeace said suddenly, looking up at her. "Yes, that's what it was. Traps and snares and suchlike."

"Well, how long should that take?"

"I don't know," he murmured. "How could I? It'll take as long as it takes."

"But -"

"I shouldn't be surprised if he stays out all night, to be honest," he added. "You know what he's like, he always wants to do things properly. The best thing might be for us both to retire."

"All night?" She was evidently astonished by this suggestion. "He never stays out all night."

"Well, perhaps he will this time," he replied, "and then... and then in the morning everything will be alright. Yes, that's certainly what will happen. He'll stay out all night and then in the morning... we'll all be able to fix things."

"Sir," she said cautiously, "forgive me for speaking out of place, but I can't help thinking that you seem to be... hiding something from me."

"Hiding something?"

"Your guests all left very suddenly," she pointed out, "and one or two of them looked at me with very pale countenances. I know that I might be letting my imagination run rampant, but I can't help worrying that they all seemed to... I just worry that they seemed to know something that I don't. Could that be the case, Sir?"

"I have no idea what you're talking about," he replied, "but -"

Suddenly they both heard a dog barking outside. As Anne turned to the window, Lord Makepeace looked toward the open doorway as the dog barked again, already sounding much closer this time.

"Thank the Lord," Anne said with a hugely relieved sigh. "They're back."

"You can't be sure of that."

"Monty never goes anywhere without his master," she said as she headed out into the hallway. "I must admit, I was starting to imagine all sorts of things that might have gone wrong, but at least they're back now. If it's alright with you, I shall prepare something for Maurice to eat. He must be absolutely starving."

"Yes, he must be," Lord Makepeace said under his breath, glancing at the clock and seeing that the time was now 1:03 in the morning, "but -"

Before he could finish, he heard a knocking sound at the door. He immediately got to his feet, just as the dog barked once more.

After waiting for a few seconds, he stepped out into the hallway. He could hear Anne working in the kitchen, but as he stared at the front door Lord Makepeace couldn't help but wonder who might have knocked. As far as he was aware, his friends were all well on their way back to London and there should be nobody else around. The longer he stared at the door, however, the more keenly he felt a sense of dread starting to spread through his body.

"Was that Maurice?" Anne called out before returning from the kitchen. Stopping, she looked at her employer. "Sir? Why are you standing there like that?"

A moment later someone knocked on the door again.

"Is that Maurice?" she asked, furrowing her brow. "Why is he knocking on the front door instead of coming round to the back?"

Walking across the hall, she reached out to open the door.

"No, don't!" Lord Makepeace gasped. "If he -"

In that moment Anne pulled the door open to reveal Maurice standing on the front step. Blood had soaked the front of his shirt yet somehow the man had managed to make his way back to the house. As he stood blankly at the threshold, his wife could only stare at him with a growing sense of horror as she tried to make sense of what she was seeing, but a few seconds later Maurice toppled forward and landed with a hard, dead thud on the floor as Anne pulled back and screamed.

"It's alright," Lord Makepeace said, watching as the scream continued and blood began to slowly spread out across the floorboards. "There's no need to make a fuss. He must have had an accident, that's all."

Still screaming, Anne dropped to her knees as the dog settled next to his master's corpse.

"Obviously he had a dreadful mishap," Lord Makepeace continued, "and somehow he made it all the way back here. That's quite an achievement, really, when you think about it. But I don't think there's any real need to make a fuss, is there? Not when it's quite clear that there's nothing we can do for him now."

Realizing that he needed to take charge, he stepped over to the body and looked down at the one remaining eye. He gave Maurice a gentle nudge with his left foot, and then he turned to look at Anne as she continued to cry out on the floor. Tears were streaming down her face and her entire body was starting to tremble with shock.

"All this crying won't do any good, will it?" Lord Makepeace suggested blankly, hoping to reason with her. "You really mustn't waste too much energy, Mrs. Wooden. After all, it won't bring poor Maurice back. Why don't you go and make yourself a nice cup of tea instead? That'll make you feel a lot better, I'm sure, and then... and then I suppose we'll have to find some way to go about cleaning all this mess up. After all, he can't stay here on the floor like this forever, can he?"

He looked back down at Maurice's corpse as Anne's scream continued to fill the air.

"We shall have to get him tidied away," he continued, "and then we'll simply move on with our lives. We can't really do anything else, can we?"

CHAPTER TWENTY-FIVE

SIX MONTHS LATER, LORD Alfred Makepeace stood in the hallway of Lotham Lodge and listened to the sound of footsteps making their way through from the other side of the house.

"All done?" he asked with a faint smile.

Stopping, Anne stared at him for a moment with barely disguised disgust before somehow managing to force a smile of her own.

"All done," she said calmly.

"Well," he continued, "I must say, I shall be sorry to see you go. Mrs. Simmonds will have a lot to live up to when she arrives tomorrow. For a while I thought your efforts would never be finished. I'm just so lucky that I found someone who could not only keep the house running but who could also produce just wonderful work. You've redecorated so very well."

"That is what you employed me for," she reminded him. "Among other things. It is I who should be grateful. After Maurice's awful accident, you did not have to keep me on, but you showed such exceptional generosity." Her smile seemed to almost flicker for a moment, as if she could barely keep it going at all. "As I mentioned yesterday, I do have one final surprise for you before I leave to take up my new position down south. You always told me that you wanted some nice stained glass here and you seemed happy with my designs and work, but there is one window that I have stopped you seeing until now."

"Yes, I'm aware of that," he chuckled. "But listen -"

"Come and see," she said, gesturing for him to follow as she made her way back through to the kitchen.

"This is all rather queer," he said under his breath, before setting off after her. "I can't imagine that many gentlemen would allow work to be carried out on their property without assenting to it first. It's a good job it's in the kitchen, otherwise I never would have -"

As soon as he reached the next doorway, he

froze. Ahead, an image of himself had been created in one part of the kitchen window, made entirely out of stained glass. Astonished by the various reds and blues and yellows, Lord Makepeace was momentarily struck dumb by a sight of such beauty as morning light streamed through into the room.

"What do you think?" Anne asked, turning to him.

"It's incredible," he admitted. "I always knew you to be a remarkable artist, Mrs. Wooden, but this is something else entirely."

Stepping into the room, he looked up at the window as sunlight glinted in the various panels.

"I put it in this room because this is where it will catch the light most effectively," she told him, watching his face as she studied his reaction with great interest. "I wanted to leave something behind that would sum you up as a man, Lord Makepeace. Something that would serve as a constant reminder to you, and to anyone who comes after you, of your life here at Lotham Lodge. Of the impact of your existence."

"And that you have done most magnificently," he replied. "Mrs. Wooden, this work will stand as testament to your own artistry for many, many years to come. And of course to my own status. You have really outdone yourself. I can only hope that your next employers appreciate you as much as I have done. But tell me, will the Archers also be commissioning your stained glass work, or are you merely going to work for them as a housekeeper?"

"I shall be a mere housekeeper from now on," she told him. "Perhaps I shall get a second wind one day, but for now I rather feel that I have made my last creation." She looked at the clock on the far wall, a little way above the empty hooks. "And now, if you will excuse me," she added, "I have a few more things to do before I close down my studio for good."

***

"It's okay, Monty," she said a few minutes later as she set her case on a bench in her workshop. Her hands – criss-crossed with tiny scratches and cuts after so much work – were trembling slightly. "We're leaving shortly and then we shall never have to return to this wretched place ever again."

The dog pawed at her leg before hurrying to the open door.

"I know, and I feel the same way," Anne continued. "A carriage is coming to take us to the village, and from there we shall secure further transportation. Soon Lotham Lodge will be nothing but a bad memory. Just give me one moment, won't you?"

Stepping around the bench, she walked over to the old furnace. Reaching out, she touched the cold metal and thought of all the work she'd completed in her time at Lotham Lodge. She had spent many happy hours working on the various stained glass windows for the house, and she knew she would never again derive so much pleasure from such work. Looking down, she saw old pieces of lead that she had discarded along with various sheets of colored glass that she had created herself but that she had ultimately not needed for her pieces.

And then, spotting one of the red pieces, she held it up so that she could see it better in the light. Turning the piece around, she felt a curious sense of achievement in her chest.

"I did it, Maurice," she whispered, thinking back to the way she'd mixed the blood into the glass. "I left a little part of you behind here. I gathered up as much of your blood as possible and I used it to create the most beautifully rich colors. And now..."

Looking back at the bench, she saw the cup she'd used to scoop up some of her husband's blood.

The plan had been fragmentary at first, not really a plan at all but more... a concept of the possibility that she might be able to do something. She'd coveted that cup of blood for days, simultaneously both captivated and disgusted every time she looked into it – and she'd looked into it a lot as the plan had continued to percolate at the back of her mind. Eventually she'd decided to give it a try, and she'd carefully added drops to the glass she blew. The rich redness had, after some experimentation, resulted in a color she'd scarcely believed could be possible. Such beauty, she'd realized, could perhaps only ever have come from something so horrific.

It could certainly never be bettered.

And as the experiment had continued, her plan – like the stained glass windows themselves – had begun to slot together, and she'd gradually locked the lead neatly between each section. Having understood that Lord Makepeace intended to forget all about her husband, she'd decided to leave part of Maurice encased in the very house itself. And although she hadn't been quite sure how that was going to work, she'd felt certain that by leaving the blood in the window's panels – and in a portrait of Lord Makepeace himself, no less – she would at least prove that such horrors couldn't be ignored. Would the result cause Lord Makepeace to fall apart under the guilt of what he'd done? She had no idea, but the idea was too tempting to ignore.

"It's not right that he was able to sweep everything under the carpet," she sneered, thinking back to the kindness in her husband's face. "I might never know *exactly* what happened to you out in that forest, my darling, but I'm certain that Lord Makepeace is hiding something. At least now, with your blood forever a part of that house, there's a chance that he won't be allowed to forget whatever he did. I can't abide the idea of that horrible man spending the rest of his life in peace. He already had to permanently move out of the main house and into the lodge, and barely anyone ever visits him. Even after the new housekeeper arrives, the old bastard will be mostly alone. And I hope that somehow you're able to give him all the nightmares he deserves."

Glancing at the window, she saw Lotham Lodge outside on the far side of the driveway.

"Make him pay, Maurice," she sneered. "Make that pathetic little -"

Suddenly letting out a gasp, she looked down and saw that she had inadvertently begun to squeeze the piece of red glass, cutting her own palm in the process. She was accustomed to small cuts from her work, of course, but this was a lot deeper;

grabbing a rag, she stemmed the flow and waited for it to end completely, while the dog stood in the doorway and let out a low whine.

"I know, I know," she murmured, realizing that he was right and that the time had indeed come to leave. She saw the stained glass portrait of Lord Makepeace in the distance, set into the kitchen window, and she felt a shudder run once more through her body. "I don't truly know what I believe in, Maurice. But if there's any chance – any chance at all – that I've helped you secure your revenge on that petty little runt of a man... then I hope you enjoy it. And I hope you make him pay for all eternity."

CHAPTER TWENTY-SIX

One hundred and eleven years later...

"NO, THIS... THIS CAN'T be real," Jonathan Pearson stammered, clutching his side as he continued to stare at the figure on the doorstep. "What are you? You're some kind of trick, you..."

As his voice trailed off, he could only stare at the mangled, bloodied remains of Maurice Wooden's face. One dead eye continued to stare out, but part of the man's head had been blasted apart, leaving crooked pieces of bone poking out from beneath the meaty flesh; Maurice's mouth was open and again he seemed to be trying to speak, yet the effort was clearly too great and finally – instead – he slowly reached out with one hand.

"No!"

In that moment, filled with panic, Jonathan slammed the door shut and threw his weight against it, determined to keep it closed. As he felt the pain surging in his side, however, he slid down until he bumped against the floor, and it took every last scrap of strength in his body to keep him from simply closing his eyes and drifting away. Convinced now that he was close to death, and with enough blood in the back of his mouth to tell him that he was bleeding internally, he realized that the world seemed to be spinning. He heard another knock on the door, but already there was only one thought filling his mind.

"Rebecca," he whispered as he saw the old telephone still on the table. "Alicia..."

He hesitated for a moment, not wanting to leave the door in case the dead gamekeeper made his way through, but finally he realized that he had no choice. Terrified that he might die without hearing his wife's voice one last time, he crawled over to the table and pulled the phone down, and then he plugged it into the wall before lifting the receiver from the cradle and starting to dial the number that was burned into his memory. He heard another knock on the door, but all he could think was that if he was going to die, he had to speak to Rebecca one last time and tell her how much he'd always loved her.

Finally he heard the phone starting to

connect, and he shifted around until he was leaning against the wall. Each second felt like a battle with oblivion, and he knew now with no doubt at all that he was close to death. His eyes continually tried to slip shut, and as he heard the ringing sound he realized that perhaps Rebecca wasn't going to answer, that perhaps she was asleep and she wouldn't hear the phone ringing in their hallway or -

"Hello?" her voice said suddenly.

Opening his mouth, Jonathan tried to speak but found that he couldn't get any words out.

"Hello?" she said again. "This is Rebecca Pearson. Is anyone there?"

"Me," he groaned, forcing the word from his throat. "Rebecca... it's me..."

"Jonathan? Where the hell have you been? I've been trying to get through to you for hours!"

"I'm sorry," he whispered.

"Jonathan, are you okay?" Her tone had changed; whereas a few seconds earlier she'd sounded angry, now the sense of concern was evident. "Jonathan, what's going on? Where are you?"

"I took a little... detour," he told her as he heard Maurice knocking on the door again.

"What's that sound?" she asked. "Jonathan, I got your messages earlier, something about a place called Lotham Lodge. Are you still there?"

"I'm so sorry."

"Listen, it's been crazy here. Rose is in the hospital, she suffered some kind of seizure so they're keeping her in for observation. And Alicia's not well, she's been having all sorts of nightmares about -"

"I love you," he said as he felt himself starting to slip away.

"Jonathan, what's happening there?"

"I'm sorry... about the paper," he continued, suddenly filled with the desperate need to be honest with her. "The presentation... I left out your part, the part about the ghosts. I was scared of being ridiculed, but now... now I know I was wrong. They're real, Rebecca. They're *so* real."

"I don't know what you're talking about," she replied. "Jonathan, we can talk about all of that later, when you get home. Are you coming home now? Are you in the car? Are you on your way?"

"I've loved you since the first moment I met you," he whispered. "I had to play it so cool, but the truth is... the moment I first saw you, I just knew that I wanted to spend the rest of my life with you."

"Jonathan, you're scaring me. I think I should call an ambulance."

"No, stay on the line," he continued, terrified by the idea that she might go – and that he would then never hear her voice again. He wanted her to remain with him until the end. "I didn't know that it was possible to love someone so much, not until I met you. I just want you to know that I'll always be with you, and if... if I can conduct one more experiment from the other side, I'll try to find a way to let you know."

"Jonathan, I'm going to call an ambulance," she said firmly, "and -"

"Daddy!" Alicia gasped, suddenly joining the line. "Are you okay?"

"Get off the line," Rebecca said firmly. "Are you on the upstairs phone? Alicia -"

"Daddy, something's wrong with Rose," Alicia continued breathlessly. "I saw her and Mummy says it was a dream but I know it wasn't. She looked really horrible, like part of her head was missing, and she kept talking about breaking some glass. Do you know what that means?"

"Alicia, get off the line immediately!" Rebecca shouted angrily, sounding as if she was close to tears now. "I'm telling you to put the phone down!"

Maurice knocked on the door again, even harder this time.

"Daddy, there's something really wrong with her," Alicia sobbed. "Are you coming home soon? Daddy, please come home."

"I don't..."

Barely able to speak now, Jonathan furrowed his brow as he heard a faint clicking sound. Turning, he saw to his horror that the door's handle was starting to slowly turn.

"I don't know that I'll be home too soon," he said finally, "but if I can find some way, I'll let you know. It might not be very obvious, you might have to be really clever to see it, but... I love you, Alicia. I'm sorry I spent so much time on my work instead of just being at home with both of you. I love you and Mummy so much. Don't ever forget that."

Hearing a clicking sound, he realized that Rebecca had cut the call downstairs, but he could still hear Alicia's breaths coming from the phone on the house's first floor.

"I know you're a strong girl," he told his daughter, worried that he was running out of time now. "Look after your mother for me, and let her look after you. You're going to need each other and -"

"Jonathan!" Rebecca shouted, having grabbed the receiver from her daughter upstairs. "Listen to me carefully, I'm going to put the phone down and call an ambulance. Then, when I've done that, I'm going to call you back and stay on the line with you until it arrives. I can't find my mobile right now so that's just how we have to do it. Do you understand? You have to stay next to the phone."

"I love you," he stammered. "Rebecca -"

"I'll be one minute!" she hissed. "Just stay awake, Jonathan!"

As he heard the call ending, Jonathan felt as

if there was no way he'd be able to stay awake for an entire minute. And then, hearing a creaking sound, he looked up just in time to see the front door finally swinging open. He told himself that there might yet be a miracle, that Patricia might have returned with help, but after a few seconds he saw instead that the dead gamekeeper was still standing outside, and a moment later the lifeless figure stepped forward, finally entering the house.

"What do you want from me?" Jonathan gasped, dropping the phone and pulling back across the hallway. "He's gone! If you're here for Lord Makepeace, he died a long time ago! His ghost was here but... he's gone now!"

Maurice's bloodied face stared back at him, before taking another lumbering step forward.

"I don't know what you want from me!" Jonathan shouted, pulling back a little further until he'd managed to haul himself all the way to the opposite wall. "Leave me alone! I'm dying anyway!"

In that moment the phone started ringing again. Although he instinctively tried to crawl back across the room, desperate to hear Rebecca's voice one more time, he stopped as he saw Maurice towering over him. Blood was dripping from the dead man's wounded face and splattering against the floor.

"What do you want?" Jonathan snarled as

the phone continued to ring loudly in the cold night air. "I can't help you! You've been dead for more than a century! I can't do anything for you!"

CHAPTER TWENTY-SEVEN

"COME ON, JONATHAN, PICK up," Rebecca muttered under her breath as she stood in the bedroom upstairs with the phone against one ear. "Damn it, answer!"

"Mummy, is Daddy okay?" Alicia sobbed, pulling on her mother's arm. "Rose said he was in trouble and he sounded really bad. Is something wrong?"

"Just give me a moment," Rebecca replied, waiting and waiting to hear Jonathan's voice on the other end of the line. "They told me an ambulance is already on its way. Someone else must have called them, but he needs to stay awake until then."

"But he's going to be okay, isn't it?" Alicia asked, with tears streaming down her face now. "Mummy, tell me that he's going to be okay.

Daddy's going to come home soon, isn't he?"

***

Letting out a low, gurgling groan, the ghostly figure of Maurice Wooden slowly reached out with one trembling hand.

"Leave me alone!" Jonathan snarled, turning and trying to get to his feet, only to immediately slump back down.

Crawling across the hallway, he finally leaned against another wall as he felt himself once again slipping away. He was having to really fight to stay conscious now; the phone was still ringing over on the other side of the room but he knew he couldn't get over there. Instead he felt as if the entire world was closing in all around him, as if his fever was ramping up and he'd lost too much blood to even think straight.

"I'm sorry," he whispered, thinking of Rebecca and Alicia back in the house. "I'm so sorry. I never should have come here."

"I'm going to call you back and stay on the line with you until it arrives," he remembered Rebecca saying as her voice swirled through his thoughts. "Do you understand? You have to stay next to the phone."

Even as he heard those words echoing in his mind, he could feel himself starting to slip away. He saw out of the corner of his eye that Maurice was slowly approaching, but this time he wasn't strong enough to even try to get away. The agony in his ribs was so strong now that it was almost taking over his entire body as it throbbed in his chest. Slowly his eyes began to slip shut.

"Are you coming home soon?" he heard Alicia's voice saying. "Daddy, please come home."

The thought of his daughter's voice forced his eyes open again, and he told himself that perhaps he could hang on for her, that he could find some way to stay awake for Alicia. For a few seconds he actually began to believe that he might find some hidden, untapped reserve of strength, but that sense quickly began to fade again. He hauled himself up until he was sitting almost upright and leaning heavily against the wooden panels on the wall, but his eyes were desperately trying to close and he knew that this time there would be no way back.

"I'm so sorry," he whispered out loud again as his eyes began to shut. "I just tried to -"

In that last moment, spotting a flicker of light and hearing the sound of a car approaching, he somehow managed to open his eyes again. Turning, he looked through the nearest open doorway and saw lights approaching the house, catching the kitchen's stained glass window, illuminating the century-old image of Lord Makepeace. He had no idea whether an ambulance had managed to reach him so quickly, but after a few seconds the headlights picked out the stained glass panels even more clearly and he saw the rich red sections.

"Daddy, something's wrong with Rose," he heard Alicia's voice stammering in the back of his mind. "I saw her and Mummy says it was a dream but I know it wasn't. She looked really horrible, like part of her head was missing, and she kept talking about breaking some glass. Do you know what that means?"

As those words went round and round in his thoughts, he continued to stare at the brightly-lit stained glass in the kitchen and he remembered something Patricia Windermere had told him earlier.

"Anne Wooden was one of the most renowned stained glass artists in the country. It's said that even after her husband died, she stayed at the lodge to finish her creation. Some even claim that her tears were mixed in with the pigments. She even had her own furnace installed right here on the estate for the duration of the project. Since Lord Makepeace was desperate to show off, he would have footed the bill – I'm quite sure that it would have been mere pocket change for him. It's said that she experimented for more than two years, determined to find the exact colors that matched her vision."

And then he heard Alicia's words again.

"She looked really horrible, like part of her head was missing, and she kept talking about breaking some glass."

Turning, he looked up at Maurice Wooden again, and in that moment he realized what must have happened. Despite the intense burning and throbbing pain in his ribs, somehow Jonathan finally managed to force himself up, and then he half stumbled and half fell through the doorway and into the kitchen. Slamming against the table, he managed to stay on his feet and began to stumble over to the window.

Reaching up, he slammed a fist against the stained glass, but he quickly found that the lead sections were holding the pieces together too firmly. He looked around, desperate to find something he could use to break them, and after a few seconds he spotted some old metal pokers in the fireplace.

As Maurice's bloodied figure reached the doorway, Jonathan stumbled around the table and grabbed one of the pokers, before making his way back to the window. Every step felt like absolute agony, but he was just about able to stop and look up once more at the red glass panels. The lights outside were constantly shifting, and a flashing blue light had been added to the mix, but he could still see the richest red color in Anne Wooden's work.

"Mr. Pearson?" Patricia's voice called out from the hallway. "Mr. Pearson, where are you?"

In that moment, feeling Maurice's cold dead hand touching his shoulder from behind, Jonathan realized that he couldn't wait. He held the metal poker up and slammed its tip against the glass, shattering the first panel and then quickly doing the same to the others. Once he'd broken all the red pieces, he kept going until he'd managed to destroy most of the window, leaving only a few shards attached to the lead, and then – as the hand on his shoulder squeezed tighter – he turned and raised the poker again.

"What do you want?" he snarled. "I told you, I can't -"

Before he could finish, he saw Patricia Windermere standing directly before him and he realized that it was now her hand on his shoulder. A moment later two paramedics stepped into the room and hurried over.

"Mr. Pearson," Patricia said cautiously, "I'm sorry I took so long but -"

As soon as he opened his mouth to answer, Jonathan felt his legs fall away from under him. Slamming down onto the floor, he let out a gasp as he tried to roll over, and now he could hear voices shouting. Hands began to pull his shirt aside and he heard the paramedics barking instructions at one another while Patricia asked questions. All that activity, however, felt as if it was taking place a world away.

Although he tried to open his mouth to speak, Jonathan finally felt himself slipping into a deep sleep. His eyes slipped shut and he realized that he was sinking into darkness, and he was barely even aware of anything that the paramedics were doing to his weakened body. He felt the occasional touch and push, and for a moment he wondered whether they might be trying to restart his heart, but he simply felt himself slipping away into a vast dark void that was already pulling his thoughts apart until they disintegrated into nothingness.

And then he saw them.

For a moment he found himself looking down from high above and seeing both Rebecca and Alicia in one of the bedrooms at home. Rebecca was holding the phone and Alicia was pulling on her arm, and somehow Jonathan could just about hear their voices echoing up to him. He tried to call out and let them know that he could see them, to tell them that everything was going to be alright, but his own voice only rang out in the air around him and he saw that they weren't reacting at all.

A few seconds later he spotted a third figure standing a little further back and he turned to see Rose staring back up at him as if at least *she* could see him.

Before he had a chance to call out again, however, the entire vision faded away to nothing and he felt himself drifting up into a vast endless void of nothing.

"Get ready!" a man's voice shouted suddenly, breaking through the veil of darkness. "Clear!"

CHAPTER TWENTY-EIGHT

SITTING IN THE OLD workshop a little way from Lotham Lodge, Patricia Windermere reached out and touched the furnace. Having long since been forgotten and left undisturbed, the furnace was so very cold to the touch, even as morning light penetrated the gloom of the space.

Stepping past the furnace, Patricia saw several of Anne Wooden's tools on one of the benches, right where they'd been left all those years earlier. Nobody had bothered to clear the workshop out, and now Patricia felt as if the place had inadvertently become a kind of museum dedicated to the events of the previous century.

As she made her way to another bench, she saw an old cup stained with some kind of dark liquid. She held it up and wondered whether this might be the last of Maurice Wooden's blood. That thought sent a shiver through her bones, but she quickly told herself that there was no need to worry too much. Ever since Jonathan Pearson had broken the stained glass window in the house, the whole of Lotham Lodge had seemed so much calmer.

Setting the cup back down, she told herself that as she neared her retirement, she should probably arrange for someone to get the place emptied.

Once she'd left the building, the workshop stood in silence. Eventually a small, spindly-legged spider made its way across the top of the furnace, stopping briefly before continuing its journey across a metal surface that had once – many years earlier – burned with such intensity.

***

As soon as his eyes began to open, Jonathan saw several blurry figures looking down at him in a brightly-lit room. He blinked, clearing his vision just a little, and then he blinked again; each time he was able to see slightly better, until finally he saw an elderly man with an alarming mustache on his right and his wife on his left.

"Jonathan, say something," Rebecca stammered with obvious panic in her voice. "Anything."

"Hey," he murmured, surprised by the croaky sound of his own voice. "What... what gives?"

"You're a very lucky fellow," the man with the mustache said. "You technically died back there in that house for about a minute. Given the amount of internal bleeding you'd suffered, it's a mir-"

He caught himself just in time.

"It's extremely *surprising*," he added, "that they were able to revive you. You must have one hell of a constitution."

Although he tried to sit up, Jonathan immediately felt an unbelievably sharp pain in one side of his chest.

"Steady there," the doctor continued. "You've got several broken ribs and a few fractures as well. They're going to take quite a while to heal. You're looking at up to six weeks or perhaps slightly longer before you start to feel more like yourself again."

"The deer," he murmured.

"The what?" the doctor replied.

"Long story," he continued, before trying and failing once more to sit up.

"Don't strain yourself," Rebecca said firmly. "Jonathan, I know you can be stubborn but you really need to listen to Doctor Taggart. You're on strict orders to rest until you're better."

"I'll leave you two to hash this out," the

doctor muttered, turning and heading to the door. "I've got other patients to see, and quite frankly most of them are just as irritating as you."

"I thought we'd lost you," Rebecca said once they were alone, with tears in her eyes. "Jonathan, there was a moment yesterday when I really thought..."

Her voice trailed off for a few seconds before she reached down and squeezed one of his hands tight.

"What were you doing in that place?" she continued. "Some random old woman started going on about a dead gamekeeper and stained glass and... I mean, it just didn't make a whole lot of sense."

"I'm still trying to figure it out myself," he admitted as he thought back to the moment when he'd broken the red panels in the window. "I think I need to read up on a few things first. For example, is it even possible to mix human blood in with glass?"

"What are you talking about?"

"I saw -"

Before he could finish, he remembered the sensation of floating above one of the rooms at home, of seeing Rebecca and Alicia and Rose down there. His wife and daughter had ignored him as if they'd had no idea he was there, but Rose... he couldn't help thinking back to the way that she'd looked up at him, and to the fact that she'd seemingly exhibited the exact same injuries as Maurice Wooden. None of that made any sense, and he wasn't ready to start going on about out of body experiences just yet, but he couldn't quite shake the feeling that he'd somehow visited his family in the exact moment when he'd briefly died.

"I saw *something*," he said finally. "Enough to assuage any doubts that were lingering after Marlstone Hall." He looked up at his wife again. "I'm sorry, Rebecca, but I wavered a little. I began to think that we got carried away last year but now... now I know it's real. There's something out there, something we don't understand. I'm not saying that every ghost story is true, because quite clearly a lot of them are nonsense, but some... just a few... I think we're really onto something and it's..."

"Terrifying?" she asked, as if she'd been struggling with the same thoughts.

"This could be an entirely new field of study," he continued, wincing slightly as the pain in his ribs began to throb once more. "We can't just blab about it to anyone. We have to approach this so carefully, Rebecca. Everything I thought I was sure about in the past... it's all shattered now."

"I know the feeling," she told him, before squeezing his hand again, "but there'll be time to deal with that soon enough. We need to tread carefully. And right now, the most important thing is that you and Rose are both okay. I just want to get you home so that we can start your recuperation properly."

"What happened to Rose?" he asked. "You said she was in the hospital too. What happened at home while I was away?"

***

"I don't know," Rose whispered, sitting in a hospital bed in another ward, staring straight ahead for a moment. "It was like I fell asleep and then I... saw things."

"What kind of things?" Alicia asked.

"I don't know."

"It's okay," Alicia said, glancing briefly at the open doorway for a moment, just as a doctor wandered past. "I won't tell Mummy and Daddy."

"I don't remember it very well," Rose admitted.

"Do you remember coming to my bedroom while you were supposed to be in here?"

"I don't know," Rose said again, before thinking for a moment. "Maybe. I'm not sure. I had this really strange dream about Jonathan, about him being in trouble. He was in a house I've never seen before and it was dark, and there were ghosts all around him. And one of the ghosts knocked on the door."

"They said he's going to be okay."

"I wish I could remember more," Rose murmured. "What happened to your face?"

Puzzled, Alicia reached up and touched her cheek, finally remembering the small cut from the plastic toy.

"It's nothing," she explained. "I mean... I'm not sure."

"If that was me," Rose replied, "then I'm sorry."

"At least you haven't had another one of those fits since you woke up," Alicia pointed out, and then it was her turn to hesitate. "I'm sorry if I wasn't very nice to you when you came to live with us. It was just a big surprise, that's all, and I'm not used to sharing Mummy and Daddy. I *do* like you, though, and I think we might be able to be friends. If you want to be."

Rose turned to her, before slowly nodding.

"I can show you some of my favorite films, if you like," Alicia continued. "I've got some good ones on DVD. I also know where Mummy and Daddy keep the scary films, so if they go out to the shop ever and leave us alone, we can watch something like that. I mean... if you want to, and you're not too scared."

"I'd like that," Rose replied after a moment of thought. "I think."

"I'll be right back," Alicia said, climbing off her chair and heading to the door. "I think

Mummy's going to come through soon and get us. The doctors said you can probably come home today, but Daddy's going to have to stay here for a bit longer."

Once she was alone, Rose looked up at the various machines that were attached to her. She watched the numbers and charts, none of which she understood, and she tried to understand everything that had happened. The doctors had used words like 'epilepsy' and 'seizure', but then they'd said that they didn't think she actually had epilepsy, so she wasn't sure what had actually happened to her; as far as she could tell, nobody else had much of an idea either.

She knew, however, that she'd sensed things happening far away, and she couldn't help but wonder whether she'd somehow left her body and had gone to try to help. She'd been filled with a fear that Jonathan was in danger, and so far she wasn't sure how she'd know that.

But she'd been right.

"This way, Mr. and Mrs. Redman," a voice said out in the corridor, stirring her from her thoughts.

Looking at the doorway, Rose saw a doctor leading a man past. A moment later a woman followed, holding the hand of a little girl who looked to be no more than four or five years old. As they passed, the girl glanced into the room and briefly made eye contact with Rose.

"Come along, Cynthia," the woman said, leading her out of sight and away along the corridor.

Leaning back in her bed, Rose thought again about the sensation of being outside her own body. She hadn't said too much to anyone, because she didn't want them to think that she was crazy, but in some way she'd been able to 'see' the stained glass window at the other house, and she'd known that there was blood in there; she'd also known, without really understanding why, that the blood-stained glass had to be destroyed to stop something terrible happening.

"Rose, how are you feeling?" Rebecca said suddenly stepping into the doorway and smiling at her. "Are you ready to come home?"

AMY CROSS

CHAPTER TWENTY-NINE

"I'VE BEEN GIVEN VARIOUS quotes for the reconstruction of the stained glass window at Lotham Lodge," Patricia said a few days later, sitting with Jonathan in the little garden at the side of the hospital. "However, upon consideration of the matter, I've decided that perhaps a simple plain piece of glass might be more appropriate. Just in case."

"Just in case there's another haunting?"

"Lotham Lodge is at peace now," she told him. "I was there just this morning and the change in the atmosphere is quite pronounced. I kept telling myself at first that I was imagining it, but no, something is different in the air. If you ask me, it's quite clear what happened. Poor Anne Wooden thought she was visiting revenge upon Lord

Makepeace with the blood in the glass, but there was a rather unintended side effect. She was also trapping the spirit of her dead husband and sort of... binding him to the house. When you broke the glass, you undid all of that and poor Mr. Wooden's soul is now free."

"That sounds... convoluted," Jonathan said cautiously, before pondering the idea for a moment. "Then again, it *would* explain everything. Apart from the ghostly deer that damn near kicked me to death."

"By all accounts Mr. Wooden was loved by the animals in the forest," Patricia replied. "I wouldn't be surprised if they sensed his pain. They quite probably came to view everyone at Lotham Lodge as evil, as part of the curse that was keeping Mr. Wooden trapped. I'm sure you were just in the wrong place at the wrong time, although I have to admit... I'm glad that I had some company."

"I bet," he said under his breath.

"I'm sorry about your car," she added. "I only made it about a mile down the road before that ruddy ditch caught me out. I was quite unharmed but the car ended up upside down. Did they manage to drag it out again?"

"They did," Jonathan said, unable to hide a sense of irritation.

"Well, that's jolly good," she said with a faint smile. "I simply decided to finish the journey to the village on foot, although obviously that added quite some time to the whole endeavor. And the nice paramedics told me that they only just got to you in the nick of time. I hate to think what would have happened if I'd taken even a moment longer to raise the alarm. You know, having tried it now, I really don't think that driving is for me."

"Probably for the best," he muttered darkly.

"I should get going," she told him as she got to her feet. "It was very nice to meet you, Mr. Pearson. I only hope that you won't take this unpleasantness as an invitation to... delve too deeply into such things."

"What do you mean?" he asked.

"When I went to Lotham Lodge," she continued, "I always felt a frisson of excitement at the thought that I might one day see a real ghost. I was so desperately keen to witness an example of the paranormal, and then finally over the last few days I witnessed enough to convince me forever. And now..."

Her voice trailed off again.

"And now I think I'd really like to leave it all alone," she added. "The idea of venturing any further along that road, of perhaps learning about things that would chill me to my bones, is no longer very appealing. It's enough to know that there does seem to be something beyond this life. I'm suddenly struck by the realization that it might not be for our foolish minds to peek behind that curtain and get too good a look. There are perhaps some things that are not for us to know."

"I'm a scientist," he pointed out. "There's no way I'm just going to walk away from this. I have to know more."

"And you're not worried about the dangers? What if you go too far? What if you encounter something that harms you or... or worse?"

"That's why our research will be carried out very carefully from now on," he told her. "Certainly much more carefully than at Lotham Lodge. We'll have proper safeguards in place."

"But -"

"You don't have to worry about us, Mrs. Windermere," he added with a faint smile, amused by her reticence. "My wife and I are both professional adults and we know how to look after ourselves. I appreciate your concern, but I think we'll be just fine."

"I hope you're right," she told him. "Oh, and I realized one other thing. The ghost of Mr. Wooden was supposed to appear at three minutes past one, according to legend, but instead it showed up exactly one hour later. It wasn't until 1916 that the clocks in this country started with this infernal daylight savings rubbish. I suppose that might explain the one hour difference, might it not?"

"An interesting thought," he admitted, "and

one that I'll definitely take into account."

"Farewell, Mr. Pearson," she replied as she headed inside. "If we meet again, I hope very much that it shall be under pleasanter circumstances."

"I couldn't agree more," he told her, just as he felt the first spots of cold rain starting to fall. "And I certainly won't be wandering unprepared into any other supposedly haunted house. From now on, I'm always going to have a plan."

***

"So when he's downstairs your father's going to be on this sofa," Rebecca said as she once again straightened the blanket she'd already folded and rearranged several times. "He's probably going to keep insisting on getting up, even though the doctor told him to rest, but he's just going to have to learn to be a good patient, isn't he?"

"What time is he coming home?" Alicia asked as she and Rose watched from the doorway.

"It should be in about half an hour from now," Rebecca explained. "You know, I'm starting to think I should have picked him up from the hospital instead of letting him take a taxi. Then again, there's so much to get ready here before he arrives. I just don't want to give him any excuses for constantly moving around the house."

"She always gets like this," Alicia said,

turning to Rose with a smile.

"Like what?" Rebecca asked. "What do I get like?"

"Nothing," Alicia replied, "just... you fuss sometimes."

"I'm not fussing," her mother insisted. "I'm just trying to make sure that everything's perfect, that's all. Of course, it'd be easier if your grandmother could pop by for a few days, but I get it, she didn't want to cancel her holiday in Sorrento." She sighed. "But it's all going to be fine, and I'm sure your dad's going to listen at least sometimes."

"See?" Alicia said again, nudging Rose. "We should call her Fussy McFussyson."

"That's not very helpful," Rebecca said firmly.

"But it's true."

"And I'm afraid you girls are going to have to help out a little more around the house while he's convalescing. Not big things, but it'd be really useful if you could keep your rooms tidier."

"You can count on us, Mummy," Alicia replied. "Can't she, Rose?"

"You can count on us, Mrs. Pearson," Rose added keenly.

"And are you sure you're feeling alright, Rose?" Rebecca asked, checking her watch before hurrying out of the room. "Do you promise you'll let me know if you feel even slightly unusual?"

"I promise."

"I might grab one more pillow from upstairs," Rebecca continued, already heading up to the master bedroom. "Just in case he needs it for his back."

"Look at this," Alicia whispered, hurrying across the room and kneeling in front of a cabinet, which she pulled open to reveal several piles of DVDs. "They think I don't know about their stash, but I do. Some of these films are really disgusting. I'm talking proper levels of gore and horror, things you could never see anywhere else. I think some of them were even banned when they first came out. Some of them are really old, and a few of them are foreign so they speak in a different language but then there's a translation at the bottom of the screen. When Mummy takes Daddy out for walks, do you want to sneak in and watch some of this stuff?"

"Definitely," Rose said, keen to make a good impression even though she wasn't a fan of horror films. Having always found them far too scary, she was really much more keen on cartoons, but she didn't want Alicia to think of her as a stupid little girl. "Let's watch the grossest ones first."

"Now you're speaking my language," Alicia said with a grin. "Come and sit here and I'll show you the covers of some of the best ones. It's so good to finally have someone to talk to about all of this!"

AMY CROSS

CHAPTER THIRTY

FOUR WEEKS LATER, AS he and Rebecca stood in the wings at another conference and waited to go out onto the stage, Jonathan reached under his jacket and winced as he felt a slight twinge of pain in his ribs.

"Are you okay?" his wife asked. "Do you need some painkillers? Are you sure it's a good idea for us to even be here?"

"I wouldn't miss this conference for anything in the world," he told her. "I've got a point to prove, and it's particularly good that about half the people in the audience were also there for the last presentation I gave."

"You really don't have to do this," she replied. "Jonathan, it's so sweet of you to make the effort but I'm worried that you might be jumping the gun slightly."

"There's not one word in here about Lotham Lodge," he said, holding up his notes. "It's the exact presentation I gave before, drawing from our work at Marlstone Hall, but with one crucial difference. This time I'm not going to leave out your section about the paranormal. This time I'm going to be brave, and I'm – we're – going to stand up there and tell everyone in that audience that we've seen real proof of ghosts."

He waited for a reply, but she seemed a little uncertain.

"I thought you'd be happier than this," he admitted.

"It's not about being happy," she said with a sigh. "I appreciate the fact that you want to make up for skipping that part last time. It's really sweet of you to try to put everything right, but we didn't have to rush at the first opportunity."

"I want to set the record straight," he told her, before leaning closer and kissing her on the cheek. In the process he felt another of flicker of pain in his still-not-fully-healed ribs. "This time, when we present our evidence about Marlstone Hall, their jaws are going to hit the ground. You wrote it all up so well and I was a total coward for not showing it last time. Today we're going to fix that and change the world."

Hearing their names being called, he turned

and saw Humphrey – the host for the day's presentations – gesturing for them both to join him on the stage.

"Here goes nothing," he said, taking a deep breath. "Let's get out there and change the world."

With that, he and Rebecca made their way onto the stage to a smattering of applause from the crowd.

"Knock 'em dead," Humphrey said, patting Jonathan on the back as he left the stage. "I bet this is going to be a real corker of a show."

***

One hour later, as the cleaners continued to stack the chairs now that the conference was over, Jonathan and Rebecca sat in continued silence over by the now-shuttered cafe. Neither of them had said anything for a while, and Jonathan was still clutching the notes he'd used during the presentation.

"Well," Rebecca said finally, "I suppose it *could* have gone worse. They didn't actually throw anything at us."

"We should probably be grateful that nobody had a gun," he replied.

"We went too far, too soon," she continued. "It's obvious now, if you look back on it. We were asking them to believe way too much. We were trying to take them way out of their comfort zones."

"We have proof," he pointed out. "We showed them our evidence."

"Evidence of something extraordinary," she replied. "They needed something more. We should never have expected them to believe it all. You were right to drop the last part when you gave this presentation without me. Up until the last part we had them eating out of the palms of our hands. Then we went into that final bit – the section that *I* mostly wrote, by the way – and they started looking at us as if we were complete morons."

"Rebecca -"

"I got heckled," she reminded him. "At a scientific conference. You don't think that's *slightly* bad?"

"I really thought we could win them over," he admitted. "I know we were asking them to believe a lot of crazy stuff, but I genuinely thought that with the evidence we presented, with the footage from Marlstone Hall and all of that other stuff, we could at least get them to consider what we were telling them." He paused for a moment, reliving some of the worst parts of the presentation. "Some of them actually laughed at us."

They sat in silence for a moment longer, each of them thinking back to the muffled groans and chuckles – not to mention eye-rolling – that had gradually spread throughout the audience during the final part of the presentation. As hard as they'd tried to convince their peers that there had indeed been ghostly activity at Marlstone Hall, they'd understood fairly quickly that they were fighting a losing battle, and by the end of the whole event they'd both begun to wish that they'd held back a little more.

"I *thought* about mentioning Lotham Lodge," Jonathan said finally. "Then again, I don't have any proof of that, either. I can't believe I didn't even think to save some of the broken glass."

"You were dying," she pointed out.

"Still, a little professionalism wouldn't have gone amiss."

Hearing footsteps, he turned and looked at the door just as Humphrey sauntered into the room carrying a half empty glass of red wine. Stopping as soon as he realized that he'd been spotted, the older man seemed momentarily frozen – as if he certainly hadn't intended to bump into anyone in that instant.

"Ah," he said cautiously, "the Pearsons. And how are you two doing? I hope you're not taking today's little disappointment to heart."

"Was it really that bad, Humph?" Jonathan asked.

"I'm not sure that I'd say it was bad, per se," Humphrey replied, clearly choosing his words with great care. "It's more that your evidence wasn't quite as compelling as it might have been. You were, after all, asking us all to believe in something that's diametrically opposed to our very core beliefs. I'm afraid a few video stills aren't ever going to cut the mustard."

"I nearly died a few weeks ago," Jonathan told him.

"A lot of people nearly die every day, but that's not really proof of anything, is it?"

"We're not idiots!" Jonathan snapped, getting to his feet. "Do you really think we'd have delivered this presentation if we weren't completely sure?"

"Let's go home," Rebecca said, standing up and tapping her husband's arm. "Mum'll be getting pretty tired soon and I'd like to pick up dinner on the way."

"I'm not saying that you're wrong," Humphrey continued. "Far from it. Personally, I've seen enough strange things to make me genuinely wonder about the possibility of... something else. Something beyond our perceptions. But you have to recognize that you're asking people to make an enormous leap. For that to be possible, you need proof that nobody can doubt. The history of paranormal research is littered with hoaxes and con jobs. Those have set an extremely high barrier. If you're right about what you've found, you need to really go for broke."

"Humphrey?" a voice called out, before

Michael Melvin stepped into the room. "Oh, hello everyone. Sorry, Humphrey, can we borrow you again for a minute?"

Humphrey hesitated before turning and heading away with Michael, leaving Rebecca and Jonathan standing all alone.

"He's right," Rebecca said finally.

"About..."

"About everything," she continued. "If we genuinely believe that ghosts are real, we need to plan our investigations much more rigorously. We need to spend time working on this project, and simply running into random haunted houses won't be enough."

"I didn't exactly run into it randomly," he replied, before sighing as he realized that this was in fact exactly what had happened.

"If this is worth doing," she added, "then it's worth doing properly. We need to pick our target sites carefully, we need to really come up with some new ways of measuring and capturing this kind of activity, and only then can we consider bringing our evidence to public attention. We're laughing stocks right now and I'm not sure our careers will ever fully recover from today's presentation, not unless we come up with some proof. Like it or not, we've passed the point of no return. We're committed now."

She hesitated, before patting him on the

shoulder and starting to lead him to the door.

"So where should we start?" he asked. "There are so many supposedly haunted houses in the world. Even just in this country alone. How do we figure out which ones are worth being studied?"

"I have no idea right now," she told him as they left the room, "but somehow I'm going to find out."

Next in this series

The Haunting of Oxendon School
(The Ghosts of Rose Radcliffe book 4)

When her mother suffers a fall and needs help, Rebecca has no choice but to head to the remote village of Oxendon. And since her husband is busy at work, she's forced to take both Alicia and Rose along for the journey.

As Rebecca tends to her mother, the two young girls explore the village and soon discover an old school next to the church. Having been abandoned for many years, Oxendon School seems like the perfect place for children to play, but they soon discover that they might not be alone after all. Something is lurking in the school, something that has been waiting a long time for its chance to emerge.

Soon Alicia and Rose find themselves drawn into a dangerous game with an entity they can't possibly understand. Rose's suppressed abilities to communicate with the dead might offer their only chance for survival, but first they must unravel the true story of a tragedy that shook the village many years earlier.

Coming soon

The Haunting of the King's Head
(The Ghosts of Rose Radcliffe book 5)

Having encountered numerous ghosts now, Rebecca and Jonathan Pearson finally set out to tackle a case together. And when they learn of the supposed haunting of a nearby pub, they think they've found the perfect location. They have no idea that they're about to experience their most terrifying case yet.

For hundreds of years, The Saracen's Head has been a quiet back-street pub in a quiet little English town. Rumors persist, however, that some of the old regulars have never quite left the building. A young boy is sometimes seen standing at the front door, and a ghostly woman dressed all in black has occasionally been spotted in the rooms upstairs. As far as the current landlord is concerned, the dead have unfinished business.

As they get to work, however, Rebecca and Jonathan soon discover that they have very different ideas about how to proceed – and about the causes of the haunting in the first place. Before long, however, they realize that this particular case has its roots in a tragedy that happened many years ago, and that the effects of this tragedy are still

AMY CROSS

Books in this series

1. The Haunting of Quist House
2. The Haunting of Marlstone Hall
3. The Haunting of Lotham Lodge
4. The Haunting of Oxendon School
5. The Haunting of the Saracen's Head

More coming soon

Also by Amy Cross

1689
(The Haunting of Hadlow House book 1)

All Richard Hadlow wants is a happy family and a peaceful home. Having built the perfect house deep in the Kent countryside, now all he needs is a wife. He's about to discover, however, that even the most perfectly-laid plans can go horribly and tragically wrong.

The year is 1689 and England is in the grip of turmoil. A pretender is trying to take the throne, but Richard has no interest in the affairs of his country. He only cares about finding the perfect wife and giving her a perfect life. But someone – or something – at his newly-built house has other ideas. Is Richard's new life about to be destroyed forever?

Hadlow House is brand new, but already there are strange whispers in the corridors and unexplained noises at night. Has Richard been unlucky, is his new wife simply imagining things, or is a dark secret from the past about to rise up and deliver Richard's worst nightmare? Who wins when the past and the present collide?

Also by Amy Cross

If You Didn't Like Me Then, You Probably Won't Like Me Now

One year ago, Sheryl and her friends did something bad. Really bad. They ritually humiliated local girl Rachel Ritter, before posting the video online for all to see. After that night, Rachel left town and was never seen again. Until now.

Late one night, Sheryl and her friends realize that Rachel's back. At first they think there's on reason to be concerned, but a series of strange events soon convince them that they need to be worried. On the outside, Rachel acts as if all is forgiven, but she's hiding a shocking secret that soon starts to have deadly consequences.

By the time they understand the full horror of Rachel's plans, Sheryl and her friends might be too late to save themselves. Is Rachel really out for revenge? What does she have in store for her tormentors? And just how far is she willing to go? Would she, for example, do something that nobody in all of human history has ever managed to achieve?

If You Didn't Like Me Then, You Probably Won't Like Me Now is a horror novel about the surprising nature of revenge, about the power of hatred, and about the future of humanity.

Also by Amy Cross

The Soul Auction

"I saw a woman on the beach. I watched her face a demon."

Thirty years after her mother's death, Alice Ashcroft is drawn back to the coastal English town of Curridge. Somebody in Curridge has been reviewing Alice's novels online, and in those reviews there have been tantalizing hints at a hidden truth. A truth that seems to be linked to her dead mother.

"Thirty years ago, there was a soul auction."

Once she reaches Curridge, Alice finds strange things happening all around her. Something attacks her car. A figure watches her on the beach at night. And when she tries to find the person who has been reviewing her books, she makes a horrific discovery.

What really happened to Alice's mother thirty years ago? Who was she talking to, just moments before dropping dead on the beach? What caused a huge rockfall that nearly tore a nearby cliff-face in half? And what sinister presence is lurking in the grounds of the local church?

Also by Amy Cross

American Coven

He kidnapped three women and held them in his basement. He thought they couldn't fight back. He was wrong...

Snatched from the street near her home, Holly Carter is taken to a rural house and thrown down into a stone basement. She meets two other women who have also been kidnapped, and soon Holly learns about the horrific rituals that take place in the house. Eventually, she's called upstairs to take her place in the ice bath.

As her nightmare continues, however, Holly learns about a mysterious power that exists in the basement, and which the three women might be able to harness. When they finally manage to get through the metal door, however, the women have no idea that their fight for freedom is going to stretch out for more than a decade, or that it will culminate in a final, devastating demonstration of their new-found powers.

Also by Amy Cross

The Ash House

Why would anyone ever return to a haunted house?

For Diane Mercer the answer is simple. She's dying of cancer, and she wants to know once and for all whether ghosts are real.

Heading home with her young son, Diane is determined to find out whether the stories are real. After all, everyone else claimed to see and hear strange things in the house over the years. Everyone except Diane had some kind of experience in the house, or in the little ash house in the yard.

As Diane explores the house where she grew up, however, her son is exploring the yard and the forest. And while his mother might be struggling to come to terms with her own impending death, Daniel Mercer is puzzled by fleeting appearances of a strange little girl who seems drawn to the ash house, and by strange, rasping coughs that he keeps hearing at night.

The Ash House is a horror novel about a woman who desperately wants to know what will happen to her when she dies, and about a boy who uncovers the shocking truth about a young girl's murder.

AMY CROSS

Also by Amy Cross

Haunted

Twenty years ago, the ghost of a dead little girl drove
Sheriff Michael Blaine to his death.

Now, that same ghost is coming for his daughter.

Returning to the small town where she grew up, Alex
Roberts is determined to live a normal, quiet life. For the
residents of Railham, however, she's an unwelcome
reminder of the town's darkest hour.

Twenty years ago, nine-year-old Mo Garvey was found
brutally murdered in a nearby forest. Everyone thinks
that Alex's father was responsible, but if the killer was
brought to justice, why is the ghost of Mo Garvey still
after revenge?

And how far will the real killer go to protect his secret,
when Alex starts getting closer to the truth?

Haunted is a horror novel about a woman who has to
face her past, about a town that would rather forget, and
about a little girl who refuses to let death stand in her
way.

AMY CROSS

AMY CROSS

Also by Amy Cross

**The Haunting of Quist House
(The Ghosts of Rose Radcliffe book 1)**

She wakes up alone in a dark house. She has no memory,
no idea who she is or where she came from. Blood runs
from a wound on one side of her head. She hears strange
sounds coming from one of the rooms upstairs. She still
doesn't remember anything, but she's starting to realize
the awful truth.

She's trapped inside a haunted house.

Not even knowing her own name, the woman starts
searching for clues. The strange sounds continue. Is she
truly alone, or are there others in the house? And if there
are others, are they friend or foe? After making her first
shocking discovery, the woman begins to fear the worst.
Time is running out. The doors and windows are sealed
shut. Nothing makes sense, but a grandfather clock in
the hallway seems to offer clues.

Who is this woman? What was she doing in the house
before she lost her memory? And even if she remembers
in time, will she be able to stop the evil that lurks in the
shadows?

AMY CROSS

AMY CROSS

AMY CROSS

BOOKS BY AMY CROSS

AMY CROSS

For more information, visit:

www.amycross.com

AMY CROSS

Printed in Great Britain
by Amazon